AN ENDURING LOVE

AN ENDURING LOVE

Jean Morrant

CHIVERS

British Library Cataloguing in Publication Data available

This Large Print edition published by BBC Audiobooks Ltd, Bath, 2007.
Published by arrangement with the Author.

U.K. Hardcover ISBN 978 1 405 64220 0

Printed and bound in Great Britain by
Antony Rowe Ltd., Chippenham, Wiltshire

CHAPTER ONE

'I've been looking forward to a real Cornish cream tea,' Elliot Wilson said as he pulled out a chair for his elderly companion and signalled to the waitress. 'In fact, I promised myself this treat as I drove down from Edinburgh yesterday.'

'Well, we've come to the right place,' Mrs Collinson said. 'It's ages since I had afternoon tea at this café. When was the last time you were in Cornwall?'

'Two years and ten months ago,' he informed her, a note of bitterness edging his words as he seated himself at the opposite side of the table.

She compressed her thin lips thoughtfully, then said, 'You must be going on thirty now?'

'Twenty-eight next, actually . . .' he began, pausing when he saw her shade her eyes and lift her head to look beyond the boundary of the café garden.

'I do believe it's the Rowe family,' she said, indicating the group of people crossing the car park with a nod of her head. 'And I see they have the child with them,' she continued, clicking her tongue as she added, 'Karenza will have her hands full now.'

Hearing the name, Karenza, brought Elliot suddenly alert, his cup halfway to his lips as he glanced up in time to see the group walk over to the far side of the car park and climb into a car. Karenza Rowe. His heartbeat quickened at the mere thought of her. He groaned inwardly as the car drove off. It was always going to be this way . . .

'Remember her?' Mrs Collinson was asking he realised suddenly. 'It's that maid from near Porthaven, once a girlfriend of yours, I recall.' She nodded her greying head and continued, 'Oh yes, broken-hearted she was when you left.'

Elliot was gazing blankly in the direction of the car park as Mrs Collinson went on to add, 'Well now, back home she is, funny old carry on that . . .'

'Yes,' he responded vaguely as memories of Karenza flooded in.

'More tea?' she offered, then noting his rather preoccupied expression enquired, 'You all right, Elliot? Nothing amiss is there?'

Giving himself a mental shake he returned his attention to the woman seated opposite. 'Sorry, Mrs Collinson, I, er, I was watching the birds. They're having quite a feed on what that coach party left.'

'Still interested in birds, heh?' Mrs Collinson chuckled, and in her strong Cornish accent remarked, 'Bit grown up for they, I'd 'ave thought.'

He shook his head and leaned towards her to say, 'Your husband was the expert on birds,

2

he taught me a lot and they have never ceased to interest me.'

'But the police wouldn't believe you had spent the day only bird-watching all they years ago, eh? Funny old business that was.'

'No, and I have your husband to thank for confirming that it was all I had been doing. Thank goodness, Mr Collinson was able to vouch for my whereabouts that day.' He shook his head slowly as he added, 'A case of mistaken identity, they said—phuh! Even so, I still intend to find out who was responsible.'

'I think that's unlikely as some time has passed since that happened.'

'But it changed everything for me . . .' he said quietly, pausing as he experienced a fresh twinge of sadness the brief glimpse of Karenza had evoked.

She cast him a concerned glance. 'Go on, Elliot, have another split,' she encouraged gently. 'You won't have had a proper cream tea for ages and there's plenty of cream left in that bowl.'

His eyes were still on the car park. 'I can remember bringing Karenza here a few years ago,' he continued, 'and now there's a child . . .'

'Yes, he's a handsome young fellow,' she commented. 'I expect they will be taking him to see the King Harry Ferry come over. All little boys love that.'

Elliot nodded and looked around him with

a heavy heart.

'I still can't believe it's almost three years since you were last here,' she said.

'I'm afraid so,' he said. 'Remember that old car my grandfather used to drive?'

She nodded. 'I have a snapshot of it somewhere, took it at King Harry Ferry when he first brought you and your parents down and showed you around.'

Elliot sighed. 'That was more than a decade ago, hard to believe, isn't it, and it must be nearly sixty years since he and the rest of the American troops left here for Normandy on Operation Overlord.'

'Yes, could be, and your grandfather was one of the lucky ones, he came back,' she said, spreading strawberry jam thickly over another fresh split.

'Fortunate indeed,' Elliot nodded, his dark eyes thoughtful. 'So many lost their lives in the D-Day invasion.'

'I expect he will have told you he was stationed near here?'

'Yes, he did mention it,' Elliot agreed. 'He liked to talk about Cornwall.'

'The place where he was billeted became a hotel, *Trewyn* is the name, though I believe there has been some strange carry on there.'

'Really? Tell me more,' he said, the name *Trewyn* capturing his attention, though for the present he decided not to mention that the hotel she spoke of was the object of this

4

journey.

She laughed. 'Take no heed, just old village gossip.'

'Sounds an interesting place,' he remarked, 'particularly as Grandfather was once there.'

'Have you seen the details of the troops leaving on the signboard over there?'

Elliot glanced over to the spot she indicated nearer to the water. 'Not yet,' he said, 'but I intend to . . .' His voice trailed off as his thoughts returned to Karenza. If he was honest with himself, *Trewyn* hadn't been the only reason he had made this journey. He'd had a secret desire to see her again and the brief glimpse of minutes ago had only served to increase his yearning.

On first sight he had deliberated over calling out to her, making his presence known, but after such a long break, what kind of welcome would he have received? And now there was this young boy to consider, which made him realise she could be married.

Karenza was delighted their afternoon had proved to be a success and her young nephew's enthusiasm for his new surroundings hadn't waned. And yet, occasionally she was aware of his sadness over the loss of his mother. Something would occur to remind him, such as her name being spoken, a magazine picture of a house similar to the one he had shared with her in Bristol, or certain television programmes they had watched together until the time came when she had become too ill to continue.

Karenza sighed. It was the same for her, losing a sister had caused her great distress, and her parents still grieved for the daughter they adored. But now they were trying to make life easier for Tom, allow him to grieve in his own way. Her parents had decided to take him on holiday in their caravan where they would ensure Tom had security and love as well as fun, although Karenza knew a week or more without him was going to be hard to bear.

She would miss the boy terribly, but she must stay behind to attend an interview, hoping it would give her work and a salary to help with the extra expense of caring for Tom.

She uttered another long sigh, recalling her father's words of only moments before when he had queried her reason for not joining them on a walk down to the beach. She hadn't had the courage to admit why she was nervous of being seen in the village and had excused herself by saying, 'I'd better start dinner but you and Mum can take him, he will enjoy it.'

He shook his head and turned in the doorway, his expression one of concern. 'Karenza, you've changed in this last couple of days.'

'No, I haven't,' she denied, managing a smile. 'But I must give some serious thought to finding employment then I can relax a little.'

After persuading him to join Tom and her

mother on their way to the beach, she headed for the kitchen. Standing by the open window to welcome the cooler air coming up from the sea she pondered over her father's remark. Perhaps he was right, she had changed, nothing had been the same since she had called in the village shop the previous day in time to hear the owner discussing Elliot Wilson with another customer.

'An old boyfriend of yours, I believe, Karenza,' Percy Latham, the shopkeeper, had remarked when she'd glanced up on hearing him mention Elliot's name. 'I'm told he be staying hereabouts, bit of a cheek.'

She'd managed to show scant interest in the news, yet she couldn't control the lurch of her heart. She remembered Elliot and his parents used to stay at Ivy Lodge, a small guesthouse owned by the Collinsons, and after leaving the shop she had taken a walk up the hill to stroll past the place in case they chanced to meet.

She had wanted to question the reason for the silence after his sudden departure almost three years ago. She'd had no word of him during the time she'd been caring for her sister, Jayne, and her young son, Tom, in Bristol, and even her parents had avoided mentioning Elliot's name.

Percy Latham's words had continued to trouble her throughout the remainder of that day. Knowing Elliot may be staying in the vicinity had kept her awake most of last night, and yet if she were to come face to face with him, what would she say? 'Hello, Elliot, remember me? We were in love nearly three years ago . . . until you were arrested,' she ended aloud, a bitter edge to her voice.

*   *   *

Seated beside the open window of his hotel bedroom, Elliot raised the binoculars he'd brought in from his car to gaze across the quiet bay. But today he ignored the sea birds, adjusting the lens to bring the cottage sheltered by trees at the foot of the hill into focus. Relieved he hadn't accepted Mrs Collinson's offer of a bed in her humble dwelling, he smiled to himself over his good fortune on acquiring a room in the Rosecliffe Hotel overlooking the small bay.

From here he would have the opportunity to watch Karenza, indulge in the fantasy of his reflections as she moved around the whitewashed cottage. He lowered the binoculars and stared thoughtfully ahead as he reflected upon what Mrs Collinson had said as he drove her back from Tolverne.

He had questioned her remark about Karenza and recalled her saying, 'Been some three or four weeks now, haven't seen her to speak to, but you know what folk are like for talking.'

Stifling his impatience he'd brushed her

8

words aside and replied, 'Merely gossip, I expect, Mrs Collinson, and rarely the truth.'

Mrs Collinson had given him one of her knowing looks. 'Mark my words, my boy, some say Karenza Rowe has been up to no good.'

He'd been too upset to allow her to continue. In fact, he almost hated Mrs Collinson for uttering such a statement. Once he had delivered her to her gate he'd felt compelled to drive quickly away, yet he was desperate to know what it was that had set the villagers' tongues wagging.

Putting aside his book, Elliot poured himself a small measure of whisky and went over to the window. It was now too dark to see much activity in the village though he could hear the voices of Saturday revellers as they left the local pub. He noticed there was an upstairs light on in the cottage, but before darkness fell he'd had the powerful lens focussed on the building and seen a man leaving, arms spread in apparent annoyance.

About an hour later the same man accompanied by an elderly lady and a fair-haired boy had returned. Karenza's parents he'd assumed, but he wasn't sure about her relationship to the child.

Elliot reflected on a long sigh. It greatly saddened him to recall that a case of mistaken identity had parted him from Karenza almost three long years ago. It had been bad enough to be accused of using his hired boat to

9

transport illegal goods from a yacht moored out in the bay, something he knew nothing of, but the resulting loss of opportunity to meet Karenza and explain had greatly upset him.

Had she really told her father she never wanted to see him again?

He paced back and forth in the room and wondered, should he have made himself known to the family this afternoon or was it wiser to wait, hoping first to waylay Karenza alone? He could explain his situation, assure her he had been proved innocent of the charge against him.

He would stress how he had tried to contact her, query the reason behind her father's words of discouragement and tell her she had been constantly in his thoughts. But he now realised he must be prepared to accept that he may have lost her affection, and seeing her with the child today had told him she could be married . . .

*   *   *

On Monday morning, Karenza kissed young Tom goodbye and helped her parents load their cases and bags into the car.

'Safe journey,' she said as her father started the engine and manoeuvred his treasured vehicle through the gate on to the narrow road when she waved them out of sight beyond the high hedgerows. She was going to miss Tom terribly.

Turning back towards the cottage she glanced up to where the Collinsons' place stood on the top of the hill and wondered if Elliot Wilson really was there. Or had the shopkeeper misunderstood what he had heard? Perhaps it was merely village gossip; and part of her hoped that's all it was. Yet, whenever she thought of Elliot, she experienced that same old yearning to see him again, particularly after she had learned he'd been cleared of the charges made against him.

At the time it had seemed like everyone was against him when even the village policeman had advised her to forget him, and her father had forbidden her to make any contact.

Going indoors, she decided her first job would be to change the bedlinen so that she could have everything clean and tidy for their return. Then, perhaps later in the week, once her interview was over, she would take the bus to Truro. She would have no need to rush back to meet Tom from nursery so could browse around the shops, maybe splash out on a new outfit, something she hadn't indulged in since coming back home.

Once her chores were completed, she made coffee and took it to the sitting-room, seating herself by the open window to stare thoughtfully over the tranquil scene. What if Elliot was in the village? She wondered, should she telephone old Mrs Collinson to ask

11

if he was staying with her? Then, to give herself time to consider again if she should enquire of Elliot's whereabouts she relaxed to drink her coffee. Of course, there was a possibility Elliot wouldn't welcome seeing her, or was it her own nervousness which held her back?

Unable to relax she decided to complete some typing she had promised to do for the vicar. Collecting the papers together she crossed over to the desk by the window to close the curtains, blocking out the strong sunlight from the computer screen. Glancing along the road as she drew the curtain over she suddenly gasped in surprise, the papers sliding from her hand. There, on the other side of the road, stood the unmistakable, tall figure of Elliot Wilson.

CHAPTER TWO

For a few moments she was motionless and simply stared at him until, as if aware he was being observed, he glanced across in her direction.

'Elliot . . .' she breathed, her hand raised in an automatic gesture, when immediately he responded with a wave.

Gathering her composure, she reached down to retrieve the papers from the carpet and hurriedly placed them on the desk before going to open the front door. When she called his name she saw him hesitate for a second before he smiled and crossed over to the garden gate.

'Elliot! This is a surprise . . .' she said, striving to control the waver in her voice as she went down the path towards him.

'Karenza,' he said softly. 'It's wonderful to see you.'

'And to see you,' she returned a little breathlessly as she took in his casual but immaculate attire. 'How are you?'

'Fine,' he said, 'and delighted to find you still here.'

Her cheeks grew slightly pink. 'Are you on holiday? How's everyone?'

He laughed. 'Hey, not so fast. Give me a moment and I'll tell you, and then you can bring me up to date with your news.'

'So why don't you come in—that is, assuming you're not on your way somewhere.'

'Well, if I'm not intruding,' he began a little hesitantly, his hand on the gate.

'Oh, no, I'm on my own at present. Were you heading anywhere special?'

'No. In fact, I was hoping I might see some of the old faces . . .'

'Hey, not so much of the old!' she cried with a laugh, then fell silent in an attempt to quell the excitement rising within her as she noticed his faint flush of embarrassment.

'Sorry, Karenza, didn't mean to offend you,' he said as he drew closer. 'Actually, you haven't changed a bit, I'd have known you anywhere.'

'You, too, I recognised you immediately,' she said, leading the way into the cottage. 'Are you down here with your parents?'

He gave a slight shake of his head. 'No, unfortunately, they both have passed away. In fact, they were involved in a road accident shortly after our last holiday here—that is, the last time we met.'

'Oh, I am sorry. They loved coming here for their holidays. And I remember your grandfather when he was alive. He knew the area well, had so many memories . . .'

'As I have, Karenza,' he said softly as he followed her into the sitting room.

For a moment Karenza was silent, then indicating an easy chair, rushed on to suggest, 'Perhaps you'd like a cool drink, it's awfully hot today.'

She saw him give a gentle shrug as she turned to go to the kitchen, willing herself to relax as she took a jug of cider from the fridge.

'How's the family?' she heard him ask as she loaded the jug and glasses on to a tray.

'My parents have gone to their caravan for a week or so,' she explained, pouring out the golden liquid, 'and they've taken Tom with them.'

'Tom? Is that your son?' he ventured.

'No, my nephew, though I've taken responsibility for him now.'

'Oh, I see.'

'Is this the first time you've been back to Cornwall since . . . well, you know, since the er, trouble?'

He raised an eyebrow, and on a slightly harsh note suggested, 'Since I was arrested do you mean?'

She glanced away, unable to meet his eyes. 'Yes, I suppose I do,' she said and rushed on to add, 'Not that I ever believed you capable of doing anything criminal.'

'But you never replied to my letters,' he reminded her, 'so I assumed you believed me to be guilty . . .'

'Oh, no!' she protested, her blue eyes widening. 'No, Elliot, you're quite wrong. I was so relieved when I heard there had been a mistake, that you had been wrongly accused.'

He gave a faint smile. 'Can I believe that, Karenza?'

'Of course . . .'

'But my letters—why didn't you reply?'

'I wasn't here. I left the day after you were taken to Truro, and my parents joined me shortly afterwards.'

He stared at her in surprise. 'Left? How do you mean, left?'

'We had an urgent call to Bristol, to my sister's home. She had been taken ill— extremely ill, actually—and as she had a young

15

baby, Tom, that is, and was resisting going into hospital, her doctor was very concerned.'

'I see. And how are things now—is she better?'

She uttered a sad little sigh and he noticed the faint quiver of her lower lip as she told him, 'No, Elliot, she died nearly four months ago.'

'Oh, Karenza, I am sorry,' he said, spreading his hands in a helpless gesture. 'So I can understand why you have taken in her child.'

'Yes, during the time we were in Bristol I grew very fond of him.' She smiled. 'He's a dear little chap.'

'But what about his father?'

Her mouth tightened as she explained. 'Unknown to my sister, he was already married and didn't want to know.'

'Well, I'm sure Tom couldn't have a better replacement for his mother. He's still with her family, and that is certain to mean something to him.' Karenza smiled and nodded. Then, fighting the tension within him he rushed on to ask, 'Incidentally, are you married?'

She appeared slightly taken aback at the suddenness of his question and simply shook her head and continued to explain. 'Jayne was critically ill, we knew she wouldn't recover. At first we considered putting this place on the market and moving to Bristol rather than upset Tom, but Jayne's house was only rented and all Tom talked about was going to live at

16

the seaside, so we decided to bring him down here.'

Elliot smiled. 'I'm so pleased about that.'

'We only came back about four weeks ago. We let this place to holidaymakers you see, so now we are trying to adjust to the change and return to our old lifestyle. I'm hoping to find employment, locally if possible, as I want to avoid travelling, which will give me more time to spend with Tom.'

He allowed her to top up his glass then looked up to remind her, 'I'm still curious to know why I had no reply to my letters, Karenza? Though I realise, in the circumstances, you would be very upset.'

'You're serious, aren't you?' she said. 'Actually, I never received any word from you. I thought you were avoiding making contact with me because of the way things turned out. It gave you an ideal opportunity to end our friendship.'

'Good lord, no!' he cried in dismay. 'Unless . . . is that what you had hoped for—a complete break?'

'Oh, Elliot, of course not. I had no desire for our friendship to end. But can you imagine how I felt—you in the hands of the police, my sister ill, and I didn't even know your home address. Quite naturally, my parents thought badly of you at the time and it was many months later before we learned the truth.'

Elliot's lip curled as he exclaimed bitterly,

'But still the real culprit goes free!'

'And yet, even after all this time you are still bitter,' she declared and saw him nod when she went on to say, 'It's understandable, I'm sure I would feel the same—though I have absolutely no idea what became of your letters.'

He shrugged. 'Actually, in desperation I rang here the following morning, but it was your father who answered and insisted you wanted no further contact . . .'

'Oh, no! Believe me, Elliot, I never said that. I suppose, due to the circumstances my father was being protective, but . . .' Lost for words she slowly shook her head.

He rose and came to stand beside her. Taking the jug from her hand, he placed it on the table as he said softly, 'You know, Karenza, if I can be sure you believe in my innocence, I'm convinced my bitterness will fade.'

'I believe you . . .' she whispered, meeting his dark gaze.

Before she could continue, he reached out to draw her closer, lowering his head to capture her lips in a gentle kiss. 'Oh, Karenza, it's wonderful to be with you again,' he murmured as their lips slowly drew apart.

'Mmm, I'm so glad you came back,' she agreed on a wavering breath. 'You know, I had no idea you'd been arrested that evening. I remember waiting by the breakwater, as we'd arranged, until it was quite dark. I thought you

18

had stood me up and it was the following morning when our local policeman came by and told me what had happened.'

'I see,' said Elliot on a long sigh. 'And what did your parents have to say about that?'

'Dad was furious, said I was to have no further contact with you, and as I was to leave for Bristol that morning there was little I could do.'

'And your father never gave you my message, or my letter?'

'No, and because I didn't hear from you, at first I thought what they said about you must be true. It was quite some time later, after my mother received a visitor from the village that I learned you'd been released but, as I told you, I didn't have your home address. I then telephoned Mrs Collinson who rather reluctantly gave me your Edinburgh address but you had moved and the new owners were unable to tell me where you could be located.'

'I do wish I'd known all this,' he said, adding with a humourless smile, 'You know, if it hadn't been for old Stan Collinson I could be still locked up.'

She looked down at her hands where they lay in his and said softly, 'Yes, but you know what they are like in the village. "No smoke without fire" they said, and it seemed nothing would convince them otherwise. It was some time later when I heard that the vicar had spoken up on your behalf.'

19

'The vicar!' he exclaimed unbelievingly.

'Yes, evidently he preached a sermon on the wickedness of gossip and how we should be more forgiving . . .'

'In my case there was nothing to forgive,' he said flatly.

'I know, and I must agree it was most unfortunate the real criminal was never discovered. I recall Doctor Smith, our local GP, saying the same.'

'Unfortunate indeed, and that is putting it mildly,' he said. 'But it has made me more determined to discover who the real criminal was.'

'I wonder if the doctor can help as I'm sure he knew something was going on. You see, he owns a boat . . .'

'I can't see how he can be of help,' Elliot broke in with a hint of scorn as he released her hands and turned away.

'Oh, Elliot, will you please listen. The doctor knows pretty well everything that goes on amongst the boat owners so why don't we pay him a visit?'

'What makes you think he'll know anything about the sort of people who deal in criminal matters?' he asked, coming back to face her.

'Like the vicar, he's experienced in dealing with every kind of human being in his working life, from saints to sinners.'

'Yes, and I expect they will include me in the latter group . . .'

'That is where you are quite wrong,' she admonished, 'and if you are going to ridicule everything I say, well . . .' She spread her hands in defeat.

He uttered a sigh of regret and reached towards her. 'I'm sorry, I don't mean to be unkind, but what can the doctor tell me that I don't already know?'

'Doctor Smith had known my sister from her childhood days so when he attended a conference in Bristol, on hearing of her illness, he decided to pay her a visit. It was when he was discussing the matter with my father that I realised he knew much more about the problem than we did.'

'The problem being me . . .'

'If you'll let me finish,' she broke in sharply. 'At first my father said he didn't wish to speak of you because of what he thought you had done, but when the doctor told him you had been proved innocent, Dad reconsidered. It seems, although suspicion lay with other boatmen, the police couldn't prove a thing.'

'But your parents no longer hold anything against me,' he said with a faintly relieved smile. And enfolding her in his arms, he queried softly, 'So, dare I hope this means our friendship can continue?' Seeing her expression soften, he added, 'I want that so very much.'

'Even with my added responsibilities?' she reminded him. 'Tom means so much to me

21

now I'd never give him up. You must understand that.'

'Of course, and although I haven't met him, I saw him briefly only yesterday.'

She shot him a puzzled frown. 'Where was that?'

'Down at Tolverne, at the café there,' he replied, returning to his seat. 'I was with my ex-landlady, Mrs Collinson, when I had a brief glimpse of someone just like you.'

'Are you staying with the Collinsons, Elliot?'

'No, I'm over at Rosecliffe. I can't garage the car at the Collinsons, so I had no other choice,' he said convincingly. 'I don't like to leave it on the roadside overnight these days. Also, now I have qualified in hotel management, I like to see how efficient other hotels are.'

'You always were interested in hotels.' She smiled. 'Are you here on holiday?'

'Not a holiday exactly, Karenza. I've an appointment in Truro on Wednesday,' he explained, but something stopped him from enlightening her further. He wanted to view *Trewyn*, the hotel for which his grandfather had bequeathed him a substantial amount of money, but Elliot didn't want to divulge his intentions to anyone, just yet.

'Oh, I see, so how long will you be staying?'

'Well now, that rather depends upon you. I came down a few days early to give myself a rest, and to capture a few old memories . . .' he admitted, 'but I expect I can stay on for the remainder of the week.'

'Oh, good!' she exclaimed, delighting him with her enthusiasm. 'I'll just have to get this interview for work out of the way and then I shall have more free time.'

He looked at her, one dark brow raised. 'What kind of work have you in mind? Are you going back to that firm of solicitors in Truro?'

'No, I had to leave when I went to Bristol.'

'I know, and I was terribly disappointed when they told me you had terminated your employment with them.'

'I do a few letters for the vicar on my computer, nothing very taxing and it has enabled me to be with Tom during his first weeks here.'

'Oh, you have a computer, do you? Perhaps you can get a little more work which you can do from home.'

'Actually, the computer belonged to my sister and I was pleased to have it. But I've warned the vicar I'm looking for something more regular. He is fairly new here and we get along very well, although he's rather worried I'll soon not be available.' She smiled. 'Actually, I think he's lonely, seems to be pleased to have my company. I still have a few more leaflets to do for him.'

'How long will it take you to complete them?'

'I did most of them yesterday so an hour

should finish it,' she told him. 'I rushed on with it as I want to have a day in Truro this week.'

'How about Wednesday? I could give you a lift. Also, it will give us an opportunity to talk, you know, catch up with things,' he offered hopefully. 'We could have lunch there,' he suggested. 'But first, how about having dinner with me tonight. The meals over at Rosecliffe are excellent,' he added persuasively, 'though, like everything else down here, there's little to do after nine o'clock.'

She laughed. 'Then you must adjust to country life again whilst you're here.'

'If you will be around, then I shall be more than happy to do that. Now, what are your plans for today?'

She puckered her lips thoughtfully. 'Perhaps I ought to get the typing out of the way before I make any plans. What time would you like me to be ready this evening?'

'Half-past seven. We can sit in the grounds until dinner, gives us more time to talk.' He glanced at his watch as he rose from the chair, suggesting, 'Let's have a quick walk down to the beach, then I'll leave you to get on with your work.'

'You never know, we may catch the doctor today. He uses his boat most weekdays and goes up river to visit some of his patients.'

'So he does his rounds by boat, does he?'

She laughed. 'Yes, he says there are not so many craft on the water during the week.'

'Then he's quite a sea dog, I can well understand how he comes to know a bit about the boats around here.'

'Oh, Elliot, you should see him when the weather's bad, you wouldn't recognise him in his storm outfit.'

The doctor was just returning to his surgery as Karenza and Elliot reached the village square. Karenza introduced them and explained who Elliot was.

Doctor Smith smiled warmly. 'Ah, yes, I remember you,' he said, noting Elliot's soft Scottish accent. 'So, what has brought you back here?'

Elliot mentioned he had an appointment in Truro, and glancing at Karenza, added, 'And I've been fortunate enough to meet up with this young lady again.'

'We first met before I went to Bristol,' she put in. 'Elliot used to come down here on holiday with his family every year.'

'Down from where, can you remind me?'

'Edinburgh,' Elliot replied. 'Rather a long drive. In fact, we used to break the journey with an overnight stop, but the roads have improved since I last came down.'

'Ah, yes, of course. You will know this area well, I expect,' he commented.

'I do, although I haven't been here for almost three years. My parents spent many holidays in Porthaven and my grandfather knew it really well as he was stationed near here in the forties,' Elliot explained.

Dr Smith nodded. 'I see. Well, I'm pleased the situation in which you found yourself on your last visit hasn't put you off the place.'

'Not at all. In fact, I believe it has strengthened my resolve to get to the bottom of the matter.'

The doctor pursed his lips a moment before he advised, 'I shouldn't let it worry you, Elliot. Better for the police to handle that kind of thing.'

'You could be right,' Elliot conceded with a sigh. 'It's such a lovely place, full of good memories. I've noticed very few changes since I was last here.'

Dr Smith smiled. 'I'm pleased to hear it.'

'Karenza tells me you use a boat to do your rounds,' Elliot remarked.

The doctor nodded. 'Some of the time. Depends if it is quicker by sea or road—and I like to get the sail up when I'm not on call.'

'I used to like to do a bit of sailing myself, Doctor, found it very relaxing.'

'Then you must join me one day,' Dr Smith offered as he turned to go, 'that is, assuming you'll have an hour or two free at the weekend.'

'Thanks, I'll make sure I'm free,' Elliot replied with enthusiasm.

The doctor wished them a pleasant day and continued on his way, leaving them to stroll downhill towards the small harbour. Leaning

26

against the wall, they looked out to sea, seeing the little flotilla of sailing boats circling round the marker buoys which slowly rose and fell in the gentle swell of the water.

'There were many boats here for last Saturday's race,' she said. 'The coloured sails show up well out there, though I expect they'll be disappointed by the lack of wind today.'

'It's quite a time since I've been out sailing.' Elliot sighed. 'Yet I used to love it when Grandfather took me with him. He and my father hired a boat.'

'Was that your American grandfather?'

Elliot nodded. 'Yes, I must have told you before. He was stationed near Tolverne, went to sea from there. He met my grandmother just before he left and then came back to ask her to marry him.' He smiled. 'So you see, I have some Cornish blood.'

'That will be why your parents liked to spend their holidays here. Are there any Cornish relatives still alive?'

'No, Karenza, no-one that I know of. I believe Mrs Collinson and my gran were close friends, and most likely that was why Stan Collinson stood by me and gave the police a good character reference.'

'Ah, yes, you did mention he had saved you from going to prison.'

'Yes, Stan went into Truro to let them know I had been in the allotment with him during all that day, including the time when our boat was brought in.'

'At least they accepted his word about you birdwatching from the cliffs?'

'Yes, Stan was a local councillor with an unblemished reputation, and as a witness's description of a man seen mooring the boat didn't fit my father, nor me, they let me go. Evidently, the boat was loaded with banknotes and cigarettes and, would you believe it, they were both counterfeit!'

'Yes, Doctor Smith once mentioned it, and it's rumoured that it still goes on.' She looked at him directly as she added, 'Even so, I think he was giving you good advice when he suggested you put it behind you.'

Elliot gave a thoughtful smile. 'Perhaps,' he murmured. 'Perhaps.'

'Coming here in different circumstances should help.'

'You could be right, Karenza, so I should stay on a bit longer.'

'Oh, good. I get on well with my parents, of course, and Tom is a little angel most of the time, but I'll enjoy the change of company . . .'

'But how about the local chaps?' he broke in to ask. 'Don't you ever go out with them—socially, I mean?'

'No, our young vicar is the only unattached male I know.'

'And you did hint that he likes your company . . .'

'Perhaps I flatter myself,' she broke in with

a laugh. 'No, he only wants his typing doing, and I must say he pays very promptly. He's suggested I do something connected with tourism such as hotel reception.'

He raised his dark brows. 'And does the idea appeal to you?' he queried, concealing a smile. Until he had been into Truro on Wednesday he still felt disinclined to mention the reason he was to meet an estate agent in case the deal fell through.

'Yes, I have enquired at the hotels locally, but they've already hired their staff for this season.' She put a finger to her lips and confided, 'I thought I might set up an agency— you know, holiday lets and country pastimes— before someone else takes up the idea.'

'That's interesting,' he said, 'and it would allow you to work from home.'

'Yes, I don't want to depend entirely on my parents, but I need the work and, as I said before, without intending to sound too mercenary, I need the cash.'

Elliot nodded. 'I see, so you would rather have something more permanent, more lucrative?'

She smiled. 'Of course, providing it leaves me time to be with Tom.'

'When do you expect him to be back?'

'Not until later next week.'

'Which means you can have a few days out with me, yes?'

She nodded. 'I'd like that.'

He chuckled. 'We must make up for the lost years, Karenza. But don't forget I have a bit of business to attend to whilst I'm here.'

'Nothing connected with that problem you had two or three years ago, I hope.'

For a moment he merely looked at her, a mysterious smile on his face before he said, 'If the transaction is successful I'll let you know, then we will celebrate. Wednesday is the day that could change my life, and possibly yours . . .'

CHAPTER THREE

Elliot drove Karenza to the Rosecliffe Hotel that evening, and once he had parked the car they took a walk round the spacious grounds. Pausing a short distance from the cliff edge he turned and raised his hand to point out a fenced area high on the hilltop behind them, explaining it was where Stan Collinson used his powerful binoculars to study birds from that elevated area.

'And I spent hours on Stan's allotment, he taught me a lot,' he told her.

'He always was such a quiet man,' she remarked with some surprise. 'I'd never have guessed bird watching to be a hobby of his, though I expect he would have a good view of the harbour and coastline from up there.'

Elliot laughed. 'Yes, excellent. On rainy days he would spend ages in that old toolshed of his, just writing notes.' He paused a moment and moved his head thoughtfully from side to side before continuing softly, 'I'd very much like to get a look at those notes . . .'

'He must have been an interesting person,' she said, 'though I didn't know him well. But his wife can be such an old gossip at times, so different from Stan.'

Taking Karenza's hand they continued their tour of the garden, pausing to relax on one of the wooden benches where they had a fine view of the shrubs and plants in bloom. About to remark on the pleasant surroundings he hesitated when he caught a glimpse of a man who appeared to be watching them from between the trees. But on a second glance the watcher had gone and Elliot brushed the incident aside as he went on to say, 'You know, Karenza, with working in the city I've missed all this. I get to the coast occasionally, out of season, but when things get busy there's little opportunity to escape the hotel.'

'Ah, yes, I've been meaning to ask. Did I hear you say you had qualified in the hotel business?'

'Your question makes me realise we have a lot of catching up to do,' he said. 'Perhaps you remember me telling you I had been offered an opportunity to go into business with my aunt?'

'Mmm, you did mention it, but nothing had been finished.'

'Well, I soon realised there could be a future in it and eventually I completed a management course. Then, unfortunately, my aunt suffered ill health, leaving me with the bulk of the work to do. Not that I'm complaining as the hard work stood me in good stead, but now my cousin, her son, has also completed his course of training and quite naturally he'd like to take control.'

He stared reflectively ahead as he continued, 'I remember my grandfather looking at a hotel not too far from here the last time he came on holiday, and he used to say if ever it came on the market it was something I should seriously consider. Its name was *Trewyn*.'

'Did you decide against purchasing it?' she broke in to ask.

He shrugged. 'After my experience with the police I was hardly in the mood to consider a business venture down here.'

'Given time, you will forget that ever happened.'

He squeezed her hand and simply smiled for a moment before replying, 'Now I can be certain of at least one friend here, I think I already have. And after giving the idea some serious thought I've decided to explore it further.'

'I see, and this meeting you are to attend on

Wednesday, any connection?'

Deciding to take her into his confidence he nodded. 'Yes, a certain business property will be discussed.' Not wishing to be overheard he lowered his voice to add, 'Just between us, Karenza, the hotel my grandfather spoke of is coming on the market.'

He watched her changing expression. 'Oh, Elliot, wouldn't that be great! Imagine you with your own hotel, particularly now you are out of work.'

He laughed. 'No, not out of work exactly, just ready to move on. As I told you, I prefer country living and I don't want to hinder my cousin. There isn't enough work for two fully qualified managers in the hotel.'

'It will be really great to have you nearer. Scotland is so far away.'

Her response delighted him. 'Just what I wanted to hear,' he said softly. 'Shall we go in for dinner?'

Seated opposite Elliot in the dining room, Karenza listened to his plans with interest as they waited for their first course to arrive. 'Actually, I'm very fortunate, my grandfather left me sufficient money for a sizeable deposit,' he told her. 'Enough to make the mortgage payments easily affordable.'

'Is it a profitable business?' she enquired in a hushed voice. 'I don't mean to pry, but I know so little about the hotel trade.'

'Well, trade in Edinburgh is fairly brisk all

year round. Cornwall may be more seasonal.' He leaned forward to continue softly, 'As a matter of fact, I'd like to encourage Europeans who may be interested in studying our culture, our way of life.'

'I could help with typing, and I'm reasonably efficient on a computer,' she offered, then her hand flew to her lips. 'Sorry. I should wait to be asked.'

'I had already thought of you, Karenza, so I may take you up on your offer. Once I've made further enquiries, you can join me when I go to view?'

'I'd love to. Any idea when that will be?'

Drawing a slim notebook from his pocket he said, 'That's simple, give me your telephone number and I'll let you know,' and he entered the figures she related. Then, tearing out a page, he wrote the number for his mobile phone and pressed it into her hand. 'There, now you can contact me whenever you wish.'

'Thanks. What time do you intend going to Truro on Wednesday?' she asked, as the waitress who was hovering nearby came to take away their plates.

'Does that mean I'm to be deprived of your company tomorrow?' he queried, sending her an entrancing smile.

Karenza's heart gave a tiny, pleasurable jolt. 'You could have dinner with me tomorrow,' she suggested, 'that is, assuming you are free.'

'I'd be delighted to join you, providing I can

bring the wine.'

*   *   *

Karenza awoke early the next morning and quickly remembered she was to check the work she had completed before delivering it to the vicar.

Casting a critical eye over the layout and design of the printed sheets she had copied on to disk before delivering, she knew she could easily take on more. She would be happy to do work for Elliot which could be done here at home and not interfere with the work she hoped to gain from the forthcoming interview.

Knocking the edges of the printed sheets in to a neat pile she slid them back into the folder and was about to set off for the vicarage when the telephone rang. Just as she expected, it was Elliot and she experienced a sudden surge of pleasure.

'Not interrupting anything, am I?' he asked, and she sensed a hint of urgency in his voice when he rushed on to say, 'Something struck me this morning concerning Stan Collinson and his diaries . . .'

'His diaries?' she echoed, frowning.

'Yes, I mentioned them last night. I told you about Stan making copious notes and I thought the local bird-life might be of interest to tourists. The doctor also referred to them yesterday so I thought I would go and pay old

35

Mrs Collinson a visit. She may have kept his diaries for sentimental reasons. Give me an hour. On my way back I'll call at the shops and get a snack for our lunch, assuming you don't mind if I join you.'

'Good idea, Elliot, and will you get a carton of cream whilst you're there. It's lovely weather so we could have tea in the garden today.'

Mrs Collinson's face lit up with a smile when she opened the door to find Elliot standing there. 'Come in, my handsome,' she invited.

He perched himself on the edge of the chair.

'What brings you here today? Are you not comfortable in that old hotel across the bay— they not feeding you well?'

'Oh yes, I'm very comfortable, thanks,' he assured her. 'Also I can garage my car which means there's less chance of anyone breaking in.'

'I know I said I'd given up the bed and breakfast trade, but I would always have found room for you, Elliot.'

'I know you would, and I appreciate that, but it's the garage I needed.'

She nodded. 'Ah yes, so you said. You've just called to see me then, heh?'

'That's right, and I've brought you a few chocolates,' he said.

'Ooh, such luxury, lad. They chocolates are

my favourites, and 'em were Stan's as well.'

'You must miss him,' Elliot sympathised, pleased her husband's name had come into conversation so soon. 'How long is it now since you lost poor Stan?'

'It will be a year come September,' she said on a long sigh. 'He thought a lot about you, lad, couldn't wait to get you in that allotment of his every summer.'

Elliot smiled over the memory. 'He taught me so much about gardening and wildlife, birds in particular.'

She rose from her chair and placed a restraining hand on his arm. 'Wait there a minute, Elliot, I've got something for 'ee . . .' she said and bustled from the room when he heard her climb the narrow staircase.

Returning minutes later, Elliot saw she was carrying a worn leather binocular case, its lid and strap stained with use. 'It's my Stan's,' she explained. 'Recognise it?' And thrusting it into his hands she commanded, 'Here, you'd better take it. Stan always thought of you as the son we never had and my nieces are not likely to take an interest.'

For a moment Elliot was speechless, swallowing hard when a lump threatened to rise in his throat. 'Oh, Mrs Collinson . . . are you sure?'

'Well, I'm not likely to take up that bird-watching game at my age,' she said with a chuckle. 'What they call it? Twitching, twitcherin, or something.'

Elliot had to smile. 'I don't know what to say,' he said, giving a slight shrug. 'I can only thank you very, very much.' Holding the case close to his chest, he added, 'I promise you I shall treasure these all my life.'

'Well then, that's that,' she said briskly.

Elliot nodded. 'By the way. May I ask if you still have Stan's diaries? He used to keep them in his shed where he wrote his daily notes about planting and what wildlife he had seen,' he reminded her. 'If they are still around I'd love to read them—that is, if you would allow me to borrow them.' Seeing her hesitate he quickly assured, 'I'll take great care of them, of course . . .'

'Ah, you mean they old books,' she chuckled. 'Well, you can have them, lad, they're no use to me. As a matter of fact you're lucky, the shed needed clearing out and I'd only just brought them home when someone broke in.'

'Broke in!' he exclaimed in surprise. 'Did they do much damage?'

'Nothing that I could see, all the tools were still there, nothing was missing.' With a slight shake of her head she went on to add, 'Someone told me they had seen that young fellow that helps in Percy Latham's shop up there, but they couldn't be sure.'

Elliot frowned. 'Really? I wonder what he was after.'

She shrugged. 'Well, Latham himself has been after it, but I shall let the shed go with the allotment so that will be the end of it. There had been a bit of thieving round here so I don't want to tempt fate.'

'And you're sure you don't want the diaries back?' Seeing her shake her head he promised, 'Then, like the binoculars, I shall treasure them.'

With the diaries almost covering the past decade enclosed in a plastic carrier and stowed in the boot, Elliot drove back down the hill towards the village.

He smiled to himself as he drew close to the road where Karenza lived, until he suddenly remembered he was to purchase sandwiches and turned the vehicle round in the direction of the shop.

'Heard you were in the vicinity,' the shopkeeper said, eyeing Elliot closely. 'How have you been keeping these last few years?'

'Just fine,' Elliot replied cheerfully.

'How long are you down here for—a couple of weeks?'

'Not sure at the moment, it depends upon a number of things,' Elliot told him. 'But for now, I'd like a couple of rounds of sandwiches if you have them.'

'I got some nice pasties,' the shopkeeper suggested. 'How about having two of they?'

'Ah yes, even better,' agreed Elliot, and then remembered the cream he'd been asked to buy. 'I'd also like a carton of cream, please.'

'Only have one quarter left, but I'll be getting another delivery tomorrow if you care to call then.'

'Thanks but we won't be here tomorrow.'

'Doing a bit of touring, are you?'

'No, we're just going out for the day, but you'll be closed by the time we return so a quarter will have to do. I assume you stock the local brand?'

Latham shot him a quick glance. 'Oh, yes, all local produce. If they visitors don't like it 'em can go back home.'

Elliot smiled to himself and joked, 'Well, as a visitor myself, I really do appreciate local produce . . .'

'Including Rowe maid?' the shopkeeper broke in with over-hearty laughter.

'Now that would be telling, Mr Latham,' Elliot returned with a grin.

'I notice you remember my name?' Latham said, taking the hot pasties from the dish his young assistant held to place them in a bag.

'Oh yes, I haven't forgotten a single thing,' Elliot replied, giving Latham a wide smile as he departed from the shop.

As he went to his car he became suddenly aware someone was calling him and turned to see a dark-haired young man come hurrying from the shop, the forgotten carton of cream in his hand.

CHAPTER FOUR

Karenza was seated in one of the garden chairs when Elliot drove up to the gate. Going out to meet him she suggested, 'Why don't we have our snack out here? The weather is far too good for us to be indoors.'

'Good idea,' he said, handing her the pasties. 'By the way, I see Latham has an assistant—didn't think there would be enough work for two.'

'I don't think he's there all the time,' she said. 'Perhaps he's only employed for the season, and he looks like a foreigner to me.'

Elliot shrugged, then sliding the carrier bag from his arm said, 'Old Mrs Collinson may be a bit of a gossip, but look what she gave me— Stan's binoculars and his diaries covering nearly all of the last ten years.'

'That was kind of her. You were hoping to get a look at them.'

He drew the binocular case out of the bag. 'Stand up and take a look through these,' he directed.

Leaving the bag of pasties on the table, Karenza rose from her chair. Coming to stand behind her Elliot brought the strap of the binoculars over her head to place them in her hands as he instructed her how to adjust the lens to suit her own eyes. 'Try focusing on the church clock,' he suggested, 'then adjust each lens in turn.'

Quite suddenly, she ducked and gave a little shriek. 'Oh, Elliot!' she cried, almost losing her balance. 'I thought that gull was flying directly towards me.'

He laughed and slid his arm round her waist to steady her. 'Don't worry, that bird is far enough away, it's just terrific magnification,' he explained. 'Tell you what, one day we'll take these glasses and mine and go birdwatching. If we see anything of interest we can make notes.'

'Better still, I have a handy little tape recorder, I'll take that.'

'That would be ideal!' he exclaimed. 'Usually I have a problem trying to keep my eye on the lens and record anything new I see.'

'Afterwards I could type the notes we make on my computer,' she offered, lifting the strap of the binoculars over her head.

'We ought to take it with us when we go to view the hotel,' he suggested.

'Is the hotel open at present?' she asked.

Elliot shook his head. 'No, it closed at the end of last year.'

'Oh, I see, I didn't realise it had been closed for so long.'

'Yes, I only found out this morning when I rang the agent in Truro.'

'When are you going to view?'

'I've made arrangements to view tomorrow

afternoon.'

She nodded. 'Where exactly did you say the hotel is situated?'

'By the river towards Saint Just. I hope you'll come along with me?'

'Yes, I would love to, and I'll remember to bring the recorder.'

'I can see we are going to have a busy day, Karenza,' he smiled, 'but right now I'm going to have a look at Stan's notes.'

Whilst Karenza brought out plates and napkins for the pasties, and poured two glasses of local cider, Elliot opened the diary at the year and month of his last visit. There, in Stan's spidery but legible hand, he found notes on the movement of birds preceding a heavy storm.

But there was no reference to his arrest or the diversion he had made, going by way of the harbour to make sure the boat had been properly tied up to suit the strong tide forecast. However, at the foot of the page, he found Stan had noted the name of Constable Hall, and the telephone number of the police station in Truro.

Deep in thought, he gazed at the page unseeingly, realising Stan would not have been aware of his detour until later that day when the constable would have told him of his arrest. Uttering a long sigh, he glanced up to see Karenza standing there, a glass of golden cider in her hand.

'Sounds as though you have all the cares in the world,' she said, smiling.

Gathering his thoughts he took the glass. 'Thanks, Karenza, it was just seeing all poor old Stan's hard work—he was meticulous about his notes.'

'Well, drink this whilst it's cool. I'll bring out the pasties in a minute.'

Smiling to himself, Elliot returned to his reading. He was curious to know if there would be any reference to his arrest and the conclusions to which Stan had arrived. Flicking back a page he saw that on the day previous to his arrest there was a note about a motor launch and tender equipped with an outboard motor out in the day at midday.

And the entry for the day following his arrest caught his interest. There was a brief reference to Elliot's release, plus a question mark after the printed word, ROSECLIFFE?

Elliot frowned. If it referred to the hotel, in what way could it have been connected to his release?

Also, there was an underlined postscript at the foot of the page to say the motor launch had left some time during the hours of darkness. This entry struck Elliot as rather strange, yet faintly amusing.

From what he could recall of Stan's interests, boats were not amongst them. He had complained of seasickness on merely a short bird-watching trip out to the island.

It was almost midnight when Elliot returned to Rosecliffe. He'd had no further opportunity to study the diaries, so left them locked in the boot of his car. But it had been a most pleasant day and Karenza had cooked a very enjoyable dinner. Tomorrow could be the day when his future would be decided and he hoped with all his heart she would be beside him in this exciting venture.

As he slid into bed these thoughts were uppermost in his mind, and they mingled with his dreams so that he woke early with an eagerness to start the day. Before going down to breakfast he telephoned Karenza to remind her to be ready for when he picked her up at half-past nine.

'May as well wait until after the traffic calms down,' he suggested.

'Don't worry, I'll be ready,' she said. 'I've got the tape recorder in my bag, but it looks like another fine day so I won't bother to take a coat.'

Switching off his mobile, he slid it into his pocket and went downstairs. Looking around, he saw that Rosecliffe Hotel was furnished in a style he would like to create for his own. Everything spoke of comfort and good quality. Finding the dining-room empty he glanced at his watch to see it was not yet eight o'clock.

Thinking he was perhaps too early for breakfast, he decided to take a stroll in the grounds, going in the opposite direction to the one he and Karenza had taken the previous evening. From that side of the hotel, they'd had a clear view of the village across the bay, whereas here at the rear of the building it was hidden from sight. A short distance away, where the land sloped steeply down to the edge of the cliff, he saw a notice warning guests it was dangerous because of crumbling rock.

Catching a glimpse of rough steps hewn into the curve of the cliff, he planned to risk a walk down to the shore when the tide was out, possibly tomorrow before breakfast.

Walking over the dewy lawn at the back of the hotel, he stopped by the railings put there to protect an unsuspecting guest from falling down the steps leading to the cellars. For a moment or two he watched the birds as they searched the ground for food. Then, about to continue his stroll, he paused, hearing a man's voice coming from somewhere below.

Leaning over the railing he looked down on the flight of damp stone steps, but when he realised the voice was growing louder and he saw a dark head appear below he ducked back out of sight.

'Oui, he come to shop,' came an accented voice from below.

'Hope 'im being back doesn't mean trouble,' was the less distinct response and Elliot immediately tensed. Could he be the subject of their conversation?

46

Hardly daring to breathe he remained still and listened. 'Right, let's have the crates and I'll see you Friday,' he heard.

Considering it wiser to move away before he was spotted, Elliot quickly retraced his steps across the lawn. He must have a word with Karenza, ask her how long Latham had been at the store which was the only one in the village.

Karenza was in the doorway of the cottage when Elliot drew the car to a halt. 'Don't get out, I'm almost ready,' she called as she propped a small bag of books against the doorstep.

Even so, he alighted and went up the path to meet her. 'If you give me that bag, I'll put it in the car.'

'Thanks,' she said, handing it over. 'I just need to bag up a few items of clothing for the dry cleaners.'

'I'll help you,' Elliot offered, returning to the cottage once he'd deposited the books in the back seat of his car.

'I promised the vicar he could have a bag of books for his charity stall,' she told him as she slid the clothes into the plastic bag he held open.

'What time is your appointment?' she enquired, putting the bag intended for the cleaners on the rear seat before she got in and fastened her seat belt.

'Not until ten-thirty so I can take you right

47

into town. If I drop you at the cleaners' first you needn't carry that bag around with you all morning.'

'Thanks, Elliot, if you can drop me off near the cathedral it is only a short distance from there. Whilst I'm here I'll buy something for a meal tonight.'

'Just enjoy your shopping, we can stop for a meal somewhere after we visit *Trewyn*.' He reached into his pocket and withdrew his mobile phone. 'Here, take this. Once I've completed all my business here I can let you know.'

'Mmm, that's a good idea,' she smiled, inspecting the small item that lay in the palm of her hand. 'I must get myself one of these.'

Returning her smile, he concentrated on the road ahead until she enquired if he'd had a satisfactory breakfast. 'Quite satisfactory, thanks,' he replied, remembering the snippet of conversation he'd heard coming up from the cellar at the rear of his hotel earlier that morning. 'Incidentally, how long has Latham been at your village shop?'

'Not sure,' she said, frowning. 'I think he was there when I went to Bristol. Yes, of course, he must have taken over the shop shortly before that. If you remember, we used to get our ice-creams from there.'

'Well, he remembered me and remarked on me being back in the village,' he said, casting her a quick sideways glance. 'Almost had me

48

forget the cream.'

Karenza declined to say that she'd heard Latham make a similar remark about Elliot before she had known for sure he was in the village again, but as they now were entering the city she let him concentrate on his driving.

As they waited in a line of traffic not far from the cathedral she drew his attention to a row of business premises. 'There's the dry cleaners,' she said. 'If you like I can jump out here. Save you having to stop again.'

'Thanks,' he said, dropping a swift kiss on her cheek as she reached back for the bag of items for the cleaners. 'I'll ring you.'

She waited until the line of traffic moved on, realising she was still smiling as she prepared to cross the road to head towards the dry-cleaning business. It was then that she realised she hadn't called at the vicarage with the books, so planned to leave them on the return journey.

Back in the street, relieved of her weighty bag, she was drawn towards a café near to the cathedral, where she thoughtfully stirred her coffee as she sifted through her thoughts. She was wondering about the welcome her parents would extend to Elliot.

She picked up a leaflet inviting bookings for fishing trips in the area, including the River Fal, and after a brief glance she tucked it into her bag in case it would be of interest to Elliot.

Back in the main street, she gazed in one or

two of the better-known shops and found she had an increasing desire to have something new to wear. After trying on a few reasonably priced garments she decided on a pretty spotted blouse and a straight skirt with matching trim. Next, she planned to look for sandals to complete the outfit.

It was turned midday before she had finished her shopping, having added a few goodies for Tom for when he returned. When an unfamiliar ringing sound reached her ears she looked round to see from where it came until she realised it came from her own bag. Smiling to herself she withdrew the mobile phone and pressed a button as Elliot had instructed, her heartbeat quickening on hearing his voice.

'Hi! Finished your shopping?' he asked.

'Yes, I've really enjoyed myself.'

'Good. Give me your location and I'll be with you in half-an-hour.'

It was a quarter-past-one when Elliot joined her. He had left the car parked by a supermarket a couple of streets away and suggested they have sandwiches and coffee in the cafeteria there before moving on.

'I hope the hotel is what you want otherwise you have had a very long journey for nothing.'

He chuckled softly as he took her shopping bag. 'To be truthful, the hotel gave me a sound reason for coming here as I have always yearned to return.'

She regarded him with surprise as he escorted her over the busy road. 'So the hotel wasn't the main reason?'

He gave her hand a squeeze. 'That was the second reason, you are the first.'

For a moment, the wave of pleasure she felt took her voice away, but as he put her bag in the boot she managed to say, 'Oh yes, I forgot to leave the bag of books at the vicarage, but I don't see them.'

'They were on the back seat,' he told her. 'The diaries are in the boot.'

'I'll drop them off on the way back, but first let me return your mobile.'

He nodded. 'I bought another for you. I'll show you how to use it later.'

Unable to recall seeing the bag of books on the back seat of the car when they left she went to look in the windows. 'I don't see them,' she frowned. 'Not that they are valuable, but that's why I thought they must be in the boot.'

Elliot came back to look. 'I put them there myself,' he said with a frown as he opened the rear door to check they hadn't fallen to the floor.

'Oh, Elliot, let's forget it. They're only old books, nothing valuable.'

'OK, Karenza, we'll go,' he said with a shrug. Inwardly he felt uneasy. He was certain he had put the bag on the back seat yet he hadn't noticed them when they set off.

After a hurried snack they drove towards the River Fal. In less than an hour they had reached the narrow lane where the hotel, *Trewyn*, was situated on one side, a short distance from the steep slope that ran down to the riverbank. The garden surrounding the hotel was sadly neglected and overgrown with bramble thorns and tall nettles lining the hedge.

'Requires some work,' Elliot commented, surveying the scene. 'The paintwork needs attention, but the roof looks sound.'

'But there are no signs to indicate it's for sale,' Karenza observed. 'When did you first hear about it?'

'Only a week ago. I rang the agent in Truro, asked him to let me have details of any vacant hotels in this area and at the same time I enquired about *Trewyn*. My grandfather used to say it would be an ideal place for me,' he told her as he stopped to lean on the wooden gates. 'It was from him that I learned this place was requisitioned during the war and some of the American troops were billeted here. Also, he met my grandmother when he was here and she had told him some tale about a secret cellar where the best wines were kept.'

'What a romantic story,' she murmured dreamily. 'And to think your grandfather once spent time in this building makes it even more special.'

'Special indeed, and it has not yet been

advertised, but as the owner is abroad the agent contacted him through someone in London.' Glancing at his watch he said, 'He should soon be here then we can have a look inside.'

'You know its name,' she said, 'and yet I don't see a sign anywhere.'

'Most likely the sign is at the front of the building . . .' Elliot paused to listen then said, 'I think I hear a vehicle coming this way now.'

Parking his car as close to the hedge as possible, the agent alighted and came over to introduce himself. 'This used to be a splendid hotel,' he said, directing their attention to the building as he unlocked the padlock on the gates. 'Indeed yes, good potential, and a very valuable property, too.'

Elliot nodded, and raising his camera to his eye commented, 'From the outside it appears to be in need of some restoration.'

'Nothing major, but let's look inside, shall we?' the agent suggested, hurrying them through the overgrown garden. 'The garden needs a little attention, I must agree, but as I previously explained, the owner was hoping to resume residence.'

'I see,' Elliot murmured as he paused to take another photograph. 'But I expect it will have been affected by damp during the winter months.'

The agent smiled confidently. 'Ah, but that is where we are very fortunate. You see, during the cooler weather the caretaker kept the heating on for an hour or two every day.'

Going from room to room, Elliot was pleased with what he saw. Six double rooms, of which four were en suite, and three singles. It was exactly the size he had hoped for. He assessed room sizes and furnishing items in useable condition, and noted others he considered would need replacing. 'Needs modernisation, new bathroom fittings,' he commented with a nod in the agent's direction, and these items Karenza included on her palm-sized recorder.

'You could extend, of course,' put in the agent, glancing through the window on the spacious garden. 'In addition to its riverside location, you have a wonderful view of the open sea from the upper floor, quite a unique situation.'

Elliot pondered a moment then nodded.

'And, considering the situation, the asking price is very low,' continued the agent.

Elliot pulled a face. 'Yes, reasonably low, but there again labour costs are extremely high these days.'

'Agreed,' said the agent, 'but if you'll take my advice you won't leave your decision too long. As I said before, the owner has decided to remain abroad, he needs the warmer climate, and he doesn't want the responsibility of this place.'

'I see,' Elliot nodded, suspecting the agent

was looking for a quick sale. 'Well, once we have seen the rest of the building I'll not keep you waiting for my decision.'

'I'll look forward to that, Mr Wilson, you have my card. And now, if we go downstairs I'll show you the rest of the ground floor.'

'I expect a building this size has cellars, yes?' Elliot enquired as they reached the lower floor.

'It had, but they were closed as the owner didn't require them. They can be opened up, I'm sure. Now, let us view the kitchen and dining-room,' he suggested, hurrying them along, 'then we'll go to the other side.'

'Oh, my goodness, the place doesn't appear to have been used for years!' Elliot exclaimed as they entered the gloomy kitchen area. 'We need total modernisation here and these items can prove to be very expensive indeed. Also, we would need to decorate throughout.'

Satisfied with what he'd seen as they completed their tour, Elliot smiled and gave a nod in Karenza's direction. Turning to the agent who was locking the main door he said, 'Of course, I will need a survey, but if that is satisfactory we can then discuss the price.'

'Something that will be completely satisfactory, I'm sure,' the agent murmured as he shook Elliot's hand. 'It is a very sound building.'

'I'm surprised no-one's wanted to take possession before now,' remarked Elliot thoughtfully. 'Or is the hotel trade around here rather poor?'

'Ah, no,' said the agent with a faint shrug. 'To be quite frank, we couldn't put it on the market until the police completed their observations.'

Elliot's eyes widened. 'The police!' he exclaimed. 'What on earth have they got to do with it?'

'Smuggling, I assume,' the agent said, lowering his voice. 'In the past few months there have been a few problems on the river.'

CHAPTER FIVE

Karenza was delighted when Elliot announced he'd have to stay at least another fortnight until the survey of the hotel had been completed. 'I'm really pleased,' she said, giving him a wide smile. 'I'd like you to meet my parents and Tom when they get back next week.'

'Assuming the surveyor gives a satisfactory report and the purchase goes through, perhaps they would like to have a look round the hotel?'

'Why don't you invite them? They know you were totally unconnected with the problem you had here, but I'm sure they'd like to hear the story from you.'

'I'll be happy to oblige,' he said. 'And if I'm to open the hotel before the season ends I'd like your father's advice on the joinery work.'

'If I know Dad, now he has retired he'll welcome something to do.'

'If I do manage to purchase *Trewyn* it will mean we're going to have a hectic few weeks. I couldn't sleep last night for making plans, nor have I had the opportunity to have another look at Stan's diaries.' Reflecting upon the notes he had read and the snippets of conversation he'd overheard at the rear of Rosecliffe Hotel the previous morning, he declined to mention they also had kept him awake.

'Until you hear something definite about *Trewyn*, I think you should relax,' she advised. 'You ought to chill out over the next couple of days.'

He grinned. 'Chill out? I'm afraid that's not too easy for me at present.'

'Why not have a day off,' she suggested. 'I've never been to the Eden Project, and I don't expect you have, so why don't we have a ride out tomorrow?'

'If you're sure we can leave the house. I'm still a bit concerned about the open kitchen window we discovered on our return from Truro last night.'

'Don't worry, Elliot. Most likely I forgot to close it properly before we left. Anyway, there was no sign of anything being disturbed.'

'Well, if you're sure,' he responded, his voice tinged with uncertainty. 'It is quite sheltered at the back, no-one would see a thief entering that way.'

'And no-one would see the window wasn't properly locked,' she retaliated with a casual shrug.'

'I suppose you are right,' he said and smiled.

'Oh yes, I must tell you this,' she began and went on to relate her telephone conversation with the vicar. 'But before I could explain about the books he said something very curious. He'd seen us carrying things out to your car yesterday morning then, when we went into the house, he saw a man take something out . . .'

'Why didn't he say something before we left?'

'He was at the other end of the street trying to put his bicycle chain back on,' she explained, 'and then he saw the man dump the bag behind a refuse bin.'

'So that's where they went,' Elliot said thoughtfully. 'I don't recall locking the car when I came back for the other bag. Did the vicar recognise him?'

She nodded. 'He thinks so, said he had a look of a man called Evers who has a boat on the river.'

Elliot raised his hand. 'Just a minute, Karenza, I'm sure the agent said the name of the caretaker was Evers. I wonder if it's the same man?'

'A coincidence, I expect, but at least the vicar got his books!' she ended with a laugh.

This was no laughing matter Elliot decided, as he realised the man Evers may have thought it was the diaries he had taken and not just a bag of old books. 'I can see I'm going to have to keep an eye on your belongings,' he teased.

'You're being very protective,' she observed, slanting him a smile.

'It's because I care for you, Karenza,' he said softly, following her from the room. Catching up with her in the doorway he brushed her hair aside to plant a kiss on the nape of her neck. Then turning her to face him he cupped her cheeks in his warm hands and kissed her until the ring of the telephone interrupted them, allowing her to take a much-needed breath.

Elliot could tell the speaker was already known to her by the way she responded to the call, but when she beckoned him to the phone he was pleasantly surprised to hear Doctor Smith on the line.

'Thought I might find you there,' the doctor chuckled. 'Curiously, when I was in the shop just now, Latham was enquiring if you were staying with Karenza.'

'Was he indeed,' said Elliot softly. 'I wonder why.'

'Just something for him to gossip about, I expect, but I didn't enlighten him. However, it prompted me to ring this number before trying Rosecliffe.'

'Thanks, Doctor, I'm becoming paranoid about that shopkeeper.'

'Actually, I'm calling to say I have a couple of hours free this afternoon so how would you and Karenza like a trip in the boat?'

'Suits me fine!' Elliot enthused. 'I assume Karenza has already agreed.'

'She has. Nothing too energetic, of course, a calm day is forecast, but I'd like to hear about the hotel you're after so see you by the harbour around three.'

Elliot felt a surge of excitement at the prospect of a boat trip. He had not been on the sea since his last holiday here when he and his father had rented a boat, and for the first time they'd also added an outboard motor. But, like today, almost the whole fortnight had been disappointingly calm when sail alone was useless so they had been glad of the engine.

Then, on their last day, a storm had been brewing, he could remember it clearly, and concerned about the boat being securely moored he had gone back to his digs by way of the harbour. He clenched his jaw over the memory. Even to this day, recalling it brought back feelings of anger and indignation over the injustice of his arrest.

Uttering a deep sigh, he looked back to see Karenza had stopped to speak to an elderly gentleman seated on the wooden bench at the roadside halfway down the hill. And when she hurried to catch up with him he managed to cast aside his bitter memories and smile.

'Sorry, I didn't mean to hold you up,' she said. 'That was Mr Tresidder, you may remember him, he lives in one of the fishermen's cottages by the harbour.'

He frowned. 'Can't say I do . . . and yet the name rings a bell.'

'He remembers your grandfather, and he knew all about your parents coming here,' she told him, continuing excitedly. 'And, would you believe it, he even remembered the day the police arrested you. According to him he had told the police you looked nothing like the men he'd seen earlier out in your boat.'

Just then they heard a car door slam and turned to see Mr Tresidder had disappeared. 'That would be his daughter picking him up,' Karenza observed. 'He said he was going to her house in Saint Mawes for tea.'

Doctor Smith was aboard his boat when they reached the harbour. 'Hope we haven't kept you waiting, Doctor,' Karenza apologised, clinging tightly to Elliot's hand as they went down the cobbled slope.

'Don't worry, I've been here only a minute or two myself. Daisy Tresidder waylaid me as I was leaving the house.'

'It was her father who kept me talking,' Karenza explained, 'and, much to my surprise, he recognised Elliot.'

'Surprised me, too,' Elliot said and he went on to relate what Karenza had told him. 'I'd like to have a word with the old chap one day,' he continued, 'see how much more he can remember.'

The doctor shook his head. 'I doubt it will do you any good now,' he said, 'just put it down to experience.'

Elliot gave him a rueful smile. 'But it's not only that, one or two other strange things have happened since I last saw you,' he said and went on to repeat the curious remark the agent had made at *Trewyn*.

'The police!' the doctor exclaimed laughingly. 'Probably trying to add a bit of mystery and glamour to the place.'

Elliot remained silent whilst the doctor brought buoyancy aids from the locker. 'I realise it is extremely calm today, but better safe than sorry.'

'Yes, I'll never forget how quickly that storm rose on my last fateful day here,' Elliot put in with a grimace. 'It was because of the storm that I came down here to ensure the boat was correctly moored.'

Deciding against mentioning the man Evers, Elliot declared, 'Well, Doctor, you're the captain. Which direction do you intend to take?'

'I need to make a visit on the other side of Saint Mawes, but I thought you may like to see that hotel you're after from a bit further up the river.'

'Great!' the younger man enthused as he felt the steady throb of the engine and noticed a faint whiff of diesel fuel. 'I don't ever recall seeing it from the water.'

'Better we've got power then, it will give you a good opportunity to look, though I haven't forgotten to take you under sail one day when there's a good breeze,' the doctor promised as the gulls wheeled and shrieked overhead. With a smile in Karenza's direction he added, 'Would that appeal to you?'

She wrinkled her nose and laughed. 'Depends how windy it is. I've seen boats out in the bay almost keeling over.'

'Perfect!' Elliot enthused, adjusting her buoyancy aid. 'Perhaps Tom will enjoy sailing when he's little older, we'll have to see.'

'You make it sound as though you intend to be around for quite some time,' Doctor Smith put in, a smile on his lips. 'Do I detect a little romance in the air?'

Karenza blushed when Elliot replied softly, 'I hope so, very much.'

It wasn't long before they turned starboard into the Carrick Roads when the doctor suggested Elliot take the helm. It was quiet on the river and Elliot ensured he kept his speed within the limit until eventually they were nearing the area where the doctor was to make his call.

'Right,' Doctor Smith said. 'I'll leave you

here. You have handled a boat before so you can take her as far as the *Trewyn* Hotel.' The doctor pointed towards the jetty. 'I suggest you drop me over there,' he said. 'See you back here in about thirty minutes. That should give you time to view your hotel, though I don't recall seeing a sign when last I was up here.'

Elliot shrugged. 'Probably it has fallen down—something that must be attended to immediately, assuming I'm taking over.'

Once Doctor Smith had disembarked, they pulled away from the jetty to continue up the river, glimpsing the tranquil scene of a waterside church through the trees surrounding it. The riverbank was heavy with tangled undergrowth and the rocks at the water's edge blackened by seaweed with the odd wreck of a boat slowly rotting away beneath the overhanging branches.

She followed Elliot's pointing finger when he drew her attention to a boathouse by the riverside, sheltered by the trees. 'Looks as though it could do with a coat of paint,' he remarked, then drew in a sharp breath to exclaim, 'Karenza, look behind it, through the trees . . . it's *Trewyn!*'

'So it is!' she cried excitedly. 'Oh, Elliot, I do hope it's going to be yours.'

He smiled. 'I hope that also means you'll welcome having me around.'

She looked up at him, her eyes shining. 'Of course,' she said, then added in a teasing voice,

'Anyway, don't forget, you promised me a job.'

'And more,' he grinned, decreasing speed where the foliage of the trees was less dense so they could view the upper part of the building beyond.

'It's quite a different view from here,' he continued more seriously. 'I'd like to have taken another look but there's no sound mooring at low tide and that slipway appears to be breaking up.'

'Those pebbles look too slippery to walk over!' she exclaimed.

He glanced at the pink canvas shoes on her feet and laughed. 'Especially in those shoes,' he said, raising his binoculars, 'and yet, it appears someone has been here. I would have thought the boathouse belonged to the hotel.'

'If it does it would be an asset, you should enquire.'

'Mmm, I will, but it's strange the agent didn't mention it.'

Elliot adjusted the throttle to hold position against the tide as they continued to look around for a little longer, making plans for the boathouse and gardens.

'Are you serious about employing me?' she queried.

'Of course, Karenza, I wouldn't have suggested it otherwise.'

'But I have an interview to attend in the morning.'

'Does that mean you are turning down my

offer?'

'No, but if you are serious it would depend on the hours you would require me to work. Also, I would have to borrow Dad's car until I got my own transport.'

'You could live in,' he ventured, one brow raised.

'But what about Tom? I can't neglect my responsibility towards him.'

'I wouldn't expect you to, he could live here as well.'

She laughed. 'That would set the tongues wagging!'

'Not if we were married,' he returned quickly.

She stared at him, her lips parting in surprise. 'Are you serious?'

'Quite serious,' he said, reaching for her hand. 'You were in my thoughts all the while we were apart.'

'Oh, Elliot, I don't know what to say, though I must admit I thought about you often. Just give me a little time to consider it.'

'Then I can only hope you come to a favourable conclusion,' he said, leaning forward to kiss her when she clung to his arm, nervous when the boat rocked slightly beneath them. 'Don't worry, you're safe,' he assured her, 'but perhaps we should make our way back, I don't want to keep Doctor Smith waiting.'

As he returned to his place at the helm she

offered, 'Tell you what, when we get back I'll open the program for *Trewyn* on the computer.'

He laughed. 'Are you telling me you have already made a start?'

'Only named a file in readiness and added a few words. We can enter the additional details from my recorder, and include the boathouse or anything else you need to discuss with the agent. I'll print you a copy for when you next meet.'

'Add a reminder about this Evers chap, will you? As I didn't bring my own laptop with me I'll be grateful for your help.' He sighed and said, 'I'm getting quite impatient to make a start, let's hope nothing goes wrong.'

Once back home, Karenza switched on her computer in preparation for adding the notes on the hotel before anything escaped their memories.

'It's a useful machine,' Elliot commented. 'Do you use it often?'

'Not really. There's some of my sister's work on it still—poetry, things like that,' she told him with a sad little smile. 'I haven't the heart to erase them.'

'I understand,' he said gently. 'It will be nice for Tom to read them when he's a bit older.' He drew up another chair beside hers, his eyes on the screen as he suggested, 'Let's enter all the ideas we have for *Trewyn*.'

'Just let me insert the disk,' she said, her

hand poised over the mouse. 'And remind me to add the query about the boathouse.' But after making a few quick moves of the cursor, she paused, frowning. 'That's strange . . .' she murmured, 'and yet I could have sworn this was the disk I used.'

Taking out the disk she examined the label and uttered a sigh of impatience. 'This one's blank, but I remember writing on the label, ready to make a start. I was sure it was here on the top.' Searching amongst papers on the desk, then in the drawer, she declared exasperatedly, 'It's not here, and yet I know for sure it was copied onto disk before I deleted it.'

'What about the work you recently completed for the vicar,' he asked with a puzzled frown, 'has that been deleted as well?'

'Yes and no,' she said and explained. 'Sometimes the vicar requires me to make small alterations so I save the work each week until I know if he needs any reprints. That is why I always make a copy in case something like this happens.'

She started searching again. 'It's here somewhere, it must be,' she said and pulled out the desk drawer. But the disk was nowhere to be found and she shook her head in dismay. 'It was right here on the desk, I know it was. Someone must have taken it!'

'But who would want to take a file of work for the vicar? They must have realised it contained nothing of interest to them.'

She frowned, then pausing for thought suggested, 'If they had opened the file they would, but in preparation for making notes for you I'd changed the name on the label to *Trewyn*.'

'I see, so it is beginning to look a little suspicious,' he said slowly, glancing round the room. 'In fact, it makes me wonder if someone did break in whilst we were in Truro yesterday. Do you mind if I go and take a look in the kitchen?'

'But nothing appeared to have been disturbed,' she pointed out, 'and I can't believe anyone here would come in just to take a disk . . .'

He hesitated in the doorway to remind her, 'Unless they were interested in the name on the label?'

Going into the kitchen Elliot crossed to the window to examine the sill where, as he expected, he found the imprint of a shoe sole—a trainer by the looks of it, and another faint mark on the far edge of the draining board.

'Yes, I can see there has been an intruder,' he said as she came up behind him. 'Now, who do you think would be interested in taking a look in a file named *Trewyn*? Have I got competition? Could it be another buyer?'

'Oh, Elliot, I have no idea. And if they expected to find details of the place they would be very disappointed, we hadn't then been to view.'

'Well, whoever it was, they must have known what to look for.'

'No, how could they . . .'

'Have you mentioned *Trewyn* to anyone?' Elliot prompted, his expression growing serious. 'Anyone at all?'

She shook her head. 'I can't believe anyone would have the nerve to take my disk.'

Elliot shook his head and gave her a gentle smile. 'Was anyone aware you were going to be out of the house for most of yesterday?'

'No, I haven't spoken to anyone but you.'

'You didn't mention it to anyone yesterday—anyone at all?'

'I spoke to a couple of shop assistants in Truro,' she insisted. 'And I wouldn't discuss it with them, or the girl in the cleaners . . .'

Seeing her expression change, he pressed. 'Have you thought of something?'

'Yes, earlier this morning the lady who lives opposite made a remark which rather puzzled me. She asked if I'd started having my provisions delivered. Naturally, I was curious and asked what gave her that idea.'

'Well, what did she say?' Elliot prompted impatiently.

'She said she thought she saw the boy from Latham's come from the back of the house yesterday afternoon and assumed he'd been making a delivery. I asked her if she was sure,

70

but she wasn't certain. She thought it looked like him, though she noticed he had a plaster on the side of his face.'

'That is interesting. That plaster could be just the proof we need.'

CHAPTER SIX

When Karenza visited the village shop as she returned from her interview the following morning, there was no sign of the young assistant. It was the owner himself who came forward to serve her. 'Good morning, Mr Latham,' she said brightly. 'I would like some of your best cooked ham please.'

'Certainly, Karenza, I have some first class ham on the bone,' he said as he went behind the counter. 'Ah, family come back from their holiday, have they?'

'No, not for another week,' she replied, smiling as she added, 'I have a big appetite.'

'Entertaining that young man of yours I expect,' he grinned. 'Still here is he?'

'Yes, still here.'

'I wouldn't be surprised if he wanted to buy a place down here,' he said casually as he slid the slices of ham on to a sheet of greaseproof paper. 'Has he ever mentioned it to you?'

'And I'll have four bread cakes, please,' she interrupted, ignoring his question.

Shooting her a faintly exasperated glance he said, 'I'll just have to get them from the back room. Haven't had time to unpack the delivery yet.'

'I notice you are on your own,' she remarked as he was going to fetch the bread. 'No assistant today?'

About to disappear into his stockroom Latham halted in the doorway, his eyes narrowing. 'Assistant?'

'Yes, the young man I've seen here. Thought I saw a plaster on his face yesterday, I was just wondering if he'd had an accident.'

Latham forced a smile. 'Oh, you mean the French lad. He's all right. Just here on a school exchange, wanted a bit of retail experience, that's all.'

'I would have thought him a bit too old to be at school,' she pursued.

'But he's at college you see. Things are different in France.'

'Of course.' She nodded, and paying for the goods she'd bought she hurried back home to relate her conversation with Latham to Elliot.

'Retail experience, my foot!' Elliot exclaimed, 'I'm sure Latham is involved in something underhand.' He shot her a quick smile and enquired, 'Tell me, how did the interview go?'

'To be frank, when they told me the hours they required me to work I didn't accept. I must keep my evenings and weekends free for

Tom.'

Elliot uttered a sigh of relief. 'Thank goodness, that's one obstacle out of the way!' he exclaimed, giving her a hug. 'What are your plans for today?'

'I should go into Truro to pick up my clothes from the cleaners,' she said.

'That's fine, and once you've done that we can call on the estate agent to enquire how the surveyor is doing now he's made a start.'

'Yes, Elliot, the sooner it's yours the happier I'll be. And I hope these other mysteries can be solved.'

'Actually, Karenza, I have a confession to make. Whilst you were out this morning, I was going over what Latham said to me when I called for pasties and cream a few days ago. I remember him saying if I wanted a large carton of cream, wait until the next day when it was delivered.'

She gave him a puzzled look. 'I don't understand. You bought some cream.'

'Ah yes, but I carelessly told him the small size would do as we would be away the following day.'

'You think he got his assistant to break in whilst we were in Truro?' she said, then reminded him, 'He doesn't understand English so what use is a disk to him?'

'But, darling, he doesn't have to admit to being fluent in English. I suspect most computer disks will be similar.'

'You could be right,' she agreed, smiling to herself over his casual endearment. 'I don't believe what Latham told me about his assistant being a French student, nor did he reply when I enquired about the plaster on his face.'

Elliot shrugged. 'We must remain alert to any unusual events. Meanwhile, let's go to the estate agent's office then come back to study those disks of yours.'

She shot him a questioning look. 'Perhaps we should have mentioned it to the police in the first instance.'

'It is something we must consider should anything else occur. Right now I want to speak to the agent.'

When they returned an hour later, Elliot told her his news. 'The caretaker at *Trewyn* was a man called Evers. Evidently he's a stocky chap with extremely light blonde hair.'

'But we don't know if he was the man who took the books until we have a word with the vicar.'

'I know, but the man provided excellent references when he took the job last December and, would you believe it, one was supplied by someone in Porthaven!'

'Here!' she cried in surprise. 'Did he say who it was?'

'No, unfortunately. I don't suppose your father would know.'

'I doubt it. In any case we were still in

74

Bristol in December. Oh yes, before I forget,' she broke in. 'Dad called last night to say they are staying on for two more days. I spoke to Tom before he went to bed, he sounded so happy.' She smiled over the memory. 'Evidently the weather is beautiful and the people in the next caravan have a young daughter so Tom has a playmate.'

He warmed to her pleasure. 'Good, I'm pleased they're enjoying themselves.'

Reaching over to kiss him she said softly, 'And I love you, Elliot Wilson.'

'Then come here,' he whispered and drew her into his arms. 'I want to kiss you again before we set to work.'

Elliot was disappointed to see what the previous week's disk revealed. 'Looks like prayers for a christening service which took place last Sunday, plus a short sermon, a few church notices, and a list of expenses for last month.' He lay back in his chair and uttered a long sigh. 'If this was the usual sort of work you did for the vicar I can think of no sound reason why anyone would want to break in for it.'

'Neither can I, so it must be connected with *Trewyn* which was the name I had given that file,' she said with a sigh of resignation.

It was late when Elliot returned to the Rosecliffe Hotel that evening. Restless and unable to sleep, he was thankful he had brought in Stan's diaries from the boot of his car. Commencing with the year following his last visit, he read through the pages of May, and saw Stan had made an entry other than the usual details about his garden or the birds.

Continuing over the next familiarly grubby page, he came to another note Stan had made regarding the motor launch at anchor in the bay and registered abroad. *Seen her here before*, he had added, followed by the question, *Birdwatchers?*

Flicking over the next page, filled mainly with details about his bean plants, there was a note mentioning that the launch had left, *No bird watching observed*, which was underlined, and described the crew as *some scruffy-looking party*.

Moving on through the pages, he found no further entries about the launch until September, exactly one year after the memorable day of his arrest. Added was the comment, *Launch here again, see May.* He lay back on his pillows, trying to remember if he had seen such a vessel out in the bay when he had gone to check the moorings of the hired boat the previous year. But he couldn't recollect seeing any other boat, he'd been too intent upon his task.

Considering it useful to make a note of Sam's entries for when he called on Mr Tresidder, he reached into the top drawer of the bedside cabinet for his notepad and pen. Not finding the pad where he expected it to be with his diary he leaned out of bed to get a better look.

But after searching through the few items the drawer contained he found they had been separated, even though he was convinced he had left them together. And on close inspection of the lower drawer it seemed to him a few more items were not in their usual places, appearing as though someone had made a hasty search of the contents.

Making the few notes he required from the diaries, he decided to have a word with Mr Tresidder as soon as possible. According to Karenza, he recalled seeing someone with Elliot's boat on the slipway on the day of his arrest. In the morning he would enquire where the old gentleman lived.

In some ways Karenza was thankful the family were away, as it gave her more time with Elliot. Even so, she missed young Tom and was looking forward to introducing them to Elliot. Also, once her parents returned she must inform them of all that had occurred in their absence and hope they would be pleased to learn of her renewed friendship with Elliot.

She sighed happily; it seemed he was quite serious about marriage and living at *Trewyn*, and she had warmed to him even more when he suggested Tom could stay as well. She closed her eyes for a moment to collect her thoughts, but could picture only Elliot's handsome face.

Glancing at her watch as she came out of her reverie, she realised it was time to get ready for the drive to *Trewyn* where she and Elliot intended to have a look at the boathouse. They would assess the amount of work required to bring it up to standard for housing a boat for the use of guests during their day. From the river the structure appeared rather hazardous to reach so he had advised suitable clothing and footwear to enable them to get a closer look when the tide was low.

When Elliot arrived a short time later he chuckled over her appearance. 'At least nobody will recognise you in that outfit!'

'You did say walking could be difficult near the riverbank so I'm wearing Mum's wellingtons and the old mackintosh she wears for picking blackberries.'

Going by way of the narrow lane that ran alongside the grounds of *Trewyn*, Elliot parked in the gateway and noted it was still padlocked. Continuing down the lane on foot, they looked back to find the hotel was soon lost from sight beyond the high hedge.

At the waterside he helped her down the steep bank on to the slimy green stones, and retaining his hold on her they scrambled along towards the boathouse.

'The place is locked,' he announced suddenly, and leaning down to examine the slipway informed her, 'and yet it has been used only recently. Look, wood splinters on the concrete, and there, along the edge, traces of maroon paint!'

'Is it possible someone else is renting the place to store their boat?'

He shrugged. 'The agent didn't mention it, perhaps I should give him a ring. I expect the other door will also be locked but perhaps we can look through that window. Actually, it is in quite good repair,' he remarked.

At the small window, Elliot rubbed his hand over the glass and peered inside but there was no boat in sight, only the winding gear to haul a boat inside. Cleaning a bigger patch on the window he took a closer look and reported, 'Now I can see a coil of rope, a bucket and hose, and more wood splinters as though somebody had been dragging a boat or some other heavy wooden object over the concrete floor.'

She struggled to stand on tiptoe beside him. 'Can I look?'

He laughingly obliged by placing his strong hands around her waist, lifting her up to the window. 'See anything else?' he queried, lowering her slowly down.

'Apart from a large roll of bubblewrap, the kind used for packing, and some brown adhesive tape, there was nothing significant.'

He took another look through the window. 'I see, you mean that roll standing by the wall at the far side.' He studied a moment then turned to suggest, 'Looks quite heavy duty stuff so it may be used to insulate this place . . . and yet, I would have thought they would need something wider for that.'

At the rear of the boathouse, as he expected, he found the door secure. 'Looks like someone's been here recently,' he remarked. 'See the footprints?'

'Why don't you ask the agent?'

'Yes, I intend to. And I'd like another look at the place so let's go back by the front of the hotel,' he suggested.

'These footprints are going towards the house,' she said and set off across the dewy grass. 'I also noticed a couple of cigarette ends by the boathouse door.'

'I'd say someone has been down here in the last twenty-four hours,' he estimated. 'Stay with me, Karenza, in case there's anyone about.'

Following the tracks as they moved cautiously through the trees they drew to a halt on the edge of the overgrown lawn where they had a good view of the hotel.

'Maybe the caretaker has been here, or the surveyor,' she suggested, struggling to keep up with his purposeful stride.

'The agent said Evers had been paid off so he shouldn't be around. And I don't suppose the surveyor would come out here just to look at the boathouse.'

Following the regular pattern left by heavy

80

footwear where it had flattened the overgrown lawn they went towards the padlocked entrance gate where the trail came to an end.

Karenza went round the car to reach the passenger side, but just beside the rear wheel she spotted a red and white packet with cigarettes protruding from the torn opening at the top. 'An American brand, I believe,' she commented.

CHAPTER SEVEN

They were parked outside an inn in the next village when Elliot made contact with the agent in Truro. 'He tells me the surveyor made a start the following day,' he related, returning the mobile to his pocket. 'However, he found the boathouse inaccessible, there was no key on the bunch to fit the locks on either door.'

Karenza raised her brows in surprise. 'Then maybe it doesn't belong to the hotel after all.'

'Oh, but it does,' he broke in. 'The agent assures me it is in the deeds.'

'Had it been rented by someone?'

Elliot shook his head. 'I suggested that, but he says there's nothing about renting in any of the documents in his possession.'

'Perhaps the key was lost ages ago. After all, there wasn't a boat in there.'

Elliot uttered a groan of frustration. 'But

that is what's so infuriating. The agent can recall seeing a boat listed in the hotel's inventory amongst some papers he discovered shortly after he got the go ahead to put the place up for sale!'

'But do you remember when we first looked round, the agent mentioned something about the police being here. I wonder what that was all about?'

'No idea, Karenza, but don't let us worry about that just now,' he said, alighting from the car. 'I don't know about you, but I'm hungry!'

The inn was quaint with lots of copper and brass hanging from the beams, and they studied the framed sepia photographs of the area with interest.

'Look at this,' Karenza cried, pointing up at one picture, 'it's *Trewyn!*'

Elliot nodded. 'So it is. It must have been taken many years ago.'

'Can you see what it says underneath? The writing is very faded.'

He half closed his eyes to peer at the picture. 'Yes, just. It says *Trewyn, nineteen twenty-one.*' He laughed as he went on to add, 'What a coincidence, it was the year my grandfather was born.'

Karenza took another look and remarked, 'I would have thought it was much older than that.'

' 'Tis, my dear,' a voice behind them

interjected, and they turned to see a well-built fellow with a florid complexion standing behind the bar. 'It be a private house until it was requisitioned by the Yanks in the early forties.'

Elliot's eyebrows rose with interest. 'Ah, I see. But I suppose it will have been renovated a few times since . . .'

'Thinking of buying the place, are 'ee?' the landlord interrupted.

'Is that official?' Elliot asked. 'I haven't seen it advertised anywhere.'

'According to one of the fellows from Porthaven it is. Overheard him discussing it with the fellow who used to be caretaker there when they were in here yesterday. I expect he hears all the local gossip in his shop.'

Wondering if the shop he spoke of was Latham's, but reluctant to divulge his own plans, Elliot shook his head. 'I expect the asking price will be too high for me,' he said. 'Know much about its history?'

'Nobody been there for some months,' the landlord replied. 'Between you and me, I heard the last owner was up to no good—bit of a racketeer.'

Elliot's eyes widened. 'Really?' he said. 'That does surprise me. I can't imagine what kind of racket could possibly go on around here.'

It appeared as though the landlord felt he had said too much when he merely shrugged and said, 'Just hearsay, mind you, nothing have ever been proved.'

Elliot had gone back to his hotel before dinner to check if his room would be available for at least another week, and hoped to catch Mr Tresidder at home. He had invited Karenza to dine with him that evening and promised to pick her up at seven. This gave her an opportunity to catch up with a few small domestic tasks and press the new blouse she was to wear that evening.

She had just switched off the iron when she heard the doorknocker. Thinking it would be Elliot she rushed to open the door, but found the man on the doorstep was not a person she recognised.

'Good afternoon, Miss Rowe,' he said with an ingratiating smile. 'Mrs Collinson asked me to collect her late husband's diaries. She said you'll know which are they.' Edging forward, he went on, 'They are of great sentimental value to her and she regrets being so hasty when Mr Wilson called.'

'Then I'm afraid she is mistaken, so I suggest you ask Mr Wilson himself,' Karenza advised firmly. 'I don't have Mrs Collinson's diaries here.'

'I've been over to Rosecliffe, but he was out. In any case, Mrs Collinson is sure he brought them here.'

Knowing Elliot usually carried the bag containing the diaries in the boot of his car, she became suspicious and asked guardedly, 'Then why didn't you leave a message for him?'

'Miss Rowe,' he persisted, 'I don't want to cause you any unpleasantness . . .'

A little unnerved, Karenza spotted her neighbour in his garden and waved to him which caused the caller to step aside to look and this gave her the opportunity to close and bolt the door.

Her heart thumping madly, she went to the window to see him retreat down the path when, reaching for her mobile phone, she keyed in Elliot's number.

It was a while before he answered and she was beginning to feel anxious until she heard his voice. 'Sorry, Karenza, I had to pull off the road,' he said. 'Is everything all right?'

After blurting out her reason for making the call she continued to keep a wary eye on the window. And when Elliot promised to be with her very shortly, she uttered a sob of relief. Seating herself behind the curtain she waited, and it was only minutes later when he drew up outside and she rushed to unbolt the door.

'Karenza, sweetheart!' he exclaimed. 'What has happened?'

'Oh, Elliot, I do wish you'd been here—he wanted the diaries.'

'Let's go inside and sit down then you can give me more details,' he insisted gently. 'Who wanted the diaries? Was it anyone you know?'

'No, he was a complete stranger,' she said and went on to relate her conversation with the man almost word for word.

'I'm going to call Mrs Collinson right now then we might learn the truth. But I'm relieved you didn't tell him the diaries are locked in the boot, although when they didn't find anything in my room I expect it will be the next place they look.'

A short conversation with Mrs Collinson quickly confirmed the caller had been to her house and told her he'd been a friend of Stan's and was keen to borrow the diaries for information about gardening.

She gave a little cry of alarm. 'Why do you think the diaries are so important? What do they contain that is of such interest to someone else?'

'I'm going to go through them again. Perhaps one contains a clue and I'm sure it will be since the year of my arrest.' He paused a moment then continued, 'Something else occurred when I went over to Rosecliffe. I spoke to the receptionist about keeping my room for another week and all seemed fine until I was about to leave, when the manager came after me to say I couldn't have the room after all.'

'Did he give you a reason?'

'Said he had already taken a booking for that room and no other rooms were available.' He gave a short laugh as he added, 'But I saw the receptionist's look of surprise and noticed he quickly removed the reservations book from her desk.'

'So that means you must leave tomorrow, how unfair. Perhaps Mrs Collinson can take you as there are no other hotels or guest houses here.'

'I think it would be wiser for me to stay with you tonight as I don't like the idea of leaving you on your own.' Seeing her look of uncertainty he assured her, 'I can sleep on the sofa tonight. Your parents will be back in a couple of days. But first, I'll bring in the diaries. Have you any room in your freezer?'

'Is this a joke,' she laughed, 'have you got something to freeze?'

He grinned. 'Yes, Stan's diaries. If I wrap them well and bury them on the bottom shelf they should be quite safe.'

'I've never heard of anyone doing that before,' she giggled, 'but if I pack the other items together there will be room.'

'I'll bring them in now. I have a few things to check before dinner but I won't be away more than half an hour.'

*   *   *

Turning in to the hotel car park, he brought the car to a halt and came round to help her alight. 'You look terrific this evening,' he said warmly and suggested, 'let's have a drink in the bar before dinner. This hot weather makes me thirsty.'

Seated in the bar, Karenza looked out on the garden whilst Elliot ordered their drinks. As she waited, from the corner of her eye, she spotted a familiar figure moving in the shelter of the trees towards the rear of the hotel. At first, surprised to see Percy Latham there she then realised he most likely did business with the management.

'Nice gardens,' Elliot remarked as he seated himself beside her. 'We could take our drinks out there if you like.'

'No, I've just spotted our local shopkeeper out there.'

'Latham, do you mean?' he queried in a lowered voice. 'I wonder what brings him here. Hardly dressed for dinner, is he?'

Karenza felt a little uneasy, and as the bar grew busy, in case they were overheard, they discussed only general topics.

'Incidentally, I had a call from Edinburgh when I came back here,' he told her, holding her gaze when he became aware of the waitress's presence. 'My aunt. She rang to ask if I was enjoying myself.'

Karenza managed to retain her composure. 'Did you tell her you would be leaving tomorrow?'

Elliot sighed. 'Yes, and I had to remind her this is the only hotel in Porthaven so she can expect me back pretty soon.' Sensing the waitress still hovered nearby he glanced behind to enquire pleasantly, 'Are you waiting to clear the table?'

When the woman coloured slightly and nodded, Elliot said, 'Then perhaps you can arrange for coffee to be sent to the lounge.'

They were seated on a comfortable settee in the empty lounge when the tray of coffee arrived. Aware the waitress would hear every word, Elliot said, 'Darling, you mustn't get upset about my leaving. I'll be back next year.'

'Will you be alone?' Karenza asked sulkily as the woman turned to leave.

He shook his head and said softly, 'I hope you're not serious, Karenza. I have no ties of that kind whatsoever.'

'Oh, good. But I must confess I was a little curious.'

Reaching for her hand he admitted, 'Naturally, I've had one or two girlfriends over the years, but, believe me, nothing serious.'

'Oh, Elliot . . .' was all she could utter as their eyes met.

Holding her gaze he said softly, 'After I first met you no-one else really mattered. You were always popping up in my thoughts which is why I came back.' His dark eyes sparkled as he searched her face a moment before he continued, 'Now I am just waiting for your answer to my proposal.'

'Oh, Elliot, I do love you so much, I can only say yes . . .'

The tender moments that followed restored Karenza's happiness. And although Elliot's manner was relaxed it had occurred to him that someone was determined he should leave the area, and it could be someone who also was determined to stop him purchasing *Trewyn*.

The next morning when Elliot went down to breakfast he paused by the reception desk and enquired of the young receptionist if she was a local girl.

'Yes, I've lived around here most of my life,' she told him pleasantly.

'That being so, perhaps you can tell me at which house a gentleman by the name of Tresidder resides?'

'Oh yes, I know who you mean, sir. Mr Tresidder lives at this end of the row of fishermen's cottages, nearest to the seawall.'

Thanking her, Elliot moved away in the direction of the dining-room. He recalled seeing the old man on the seat near the row of white painted cottages and planned to call there immediately after breakfast.

Mr Tresidder was delighted to see Elliot and quickly ushered him into the cottage. 'I was hoping you'd be coming along,' he said. 'Sit yourself down.'

'Thanks, I will,' Elliot said, ducking his head as he entered and took the worn but comfortable looking chair to one side of the old-fashioned fireplace.

Seated opposite, Mr Tresidder reached for his pipe and matches that were lined up on the end of the brass fender. 'I spoke to young Karenza the other day and she tells me you be staying for a week or two.'

'Well, maybe another week or so, it depends how things go,' Elliot told him. 'Actually, I was hoping to have a word with you about *Trewyn*.'

'I've heard it's coming up for sale again so I assume that's why you're here,' Tresidder suggested with a speculative twinkle in his eye.

'I only learned of this less than a couple of weeks ago when I rang an agent in Truro and by coincidence *Trewyn* happened to be coming on the market.'

'That was a stroke of luck,' Tresidder said between puffs as he stoked up his pipe. 'I remember your father showing an interest in the place when last you were here, but after that carry on with the police and then the threats . . .'

Alerted, Elliot came upright in his seat. 'Threats did you say?' he broke in. 'I'm sorry to interrupt you, Mr Tresidder, but it's the first I've heard about this. My father never mentioned it to me.'

The old man's expression grew serious. 'Oh yes, they were threats all right, and they were against you, but he didn't want to worry you. He was going to bring the matter to the attention of the authorities once he'd got you home but, unfortunately . . .' he shrugged.

'Well, you know what happened soon after that, his accident, a terrible thing.'

'Yes, neither he nor my mother survived the crash,' Elliot supplied sadly.

Tresidder nodded. 'Well, soon after that, someone else took over *Trewyn*.'

'That hasn't lasted long—I hope it's not an omen,' Elliot said with a mirthless smile. 'I understand the owner has been very ill.'

'As I believe,' Tresidder agreed, brushing ash from the front of his waistcoat, 'which is why he moved abroad a few years ago. The last fellow only rented it, but I don't think he ran it as an hotel.'

Elliot nodded. 'Now I'm beginning to understand. The agent led me to assume it was the owner, not the tenant, who left at the end of last year.'

'That being so, you'd do well to get a bid in straight away.'

'Yes, I already have. But first can we go back to the threats my father had. Who threatened him, and why? I believe it was my grandfather you were more friendly with.'

'Yes, we were great pals,' Tresidder chuckled. 'You see, he always wanted you to have *Trewyn* because it was where he met Winifred, sentimental old fool . . .'

'Winifred, my grandmother.'

'That's right. I knew your father too, of course, but not quite so well.'

'Ah yes, my father,' Elliot prompted. 'What

were these threats about?'

'It was the night before you were arrested, he'd been making enquiries about *Trewyn*. But when he got back to Collinson's place someone telephoned to suggest it was time he went back to his own part of the country and to warn him off *Trewyn*, otherwise you would suffer.'

'So, Mr Tresidder, I gather from that, my father had already shown an interest in *Trewyn*, but someone else was opposed to the idea.'

Tresidder nodded. 'Once you had become involved in the hotel business both Greg and your father were keen to get you started.'

'And it appears there's still someone who is just as keen to prevent me buying the place,' Elliot remarked thoughtfully.

'I can tell you have your heart set on living down here. Even poor old Stan Collinson always said you'd be back.'

'I was grateful to both you and Stan for speaking out in my defence, Mr Tresidder,' he declared, 'and I do intend to stay. However, there was just one more thing I meant to ask you. You will recall the night I was arrested, but can you remember what that fellow on our boat looked like?'

Tresidder thought for a moment, then said, 'Well, as I told the police the next day, for one thing he didn't have your dark hair, and even though he was wearing one of those knitted sorts of hats I could see he was fair. In fact, very fair, even lighter than Karenza's, and he was much heavier than either you or your father.'

'But you didn't recognise him—it wasn't a local man?'

'No, not a local, Elliot, but by the way he handled that boat it was obvious he was used to it, and there were two of them when they first came in—him and a shorter dark-skinned chap. I'd first noticed them earlier having trouble with an outboard which they abandoned out on the rocks, and it's my guess it was then that they borrowed yours, transferred their cargo, then picked up another fellow who towed theirs in on return.'

'Did you say cargo?'

'Well, a wooden box or two, nothing really big.'

'Interesting,' said Elliot thoughtfully. 'We didn't go to sea that day as we were packing ready to leave early the following morning. Also, there had been warnings of an approaching storm.'

'Well, I don't suppose it would have worried them,' Tresidder snorted. 'They only went out to a motor launch in the bay. Could have been a foreigner—Dutch, French—I'm not sure, but something strange was going on.'

'Ah yes, the launch,' Elliot nodded. 'Mrs Collinson was kind enough to let me have Stan's diaries and I saw he had made a note about it. Do you think it's anything to do with smuggling?'

Tresidder nodded. 'We both thought so, and Stan kept a diary, though he used to tell folk it were for keeping a record of his vegetables and observations of birds. There again, you would do well to look closer as he told me he had noticed some queer goings on last September. It was his intention to bring it to the notice of the coastguard, but of course it was September when he died, poor chap.'

CHAPTER EIGHT

'Why not let me help you?' Karenza suggested when she made coffee for Elliot.

'Right, you're on,' he said, delving into the carrier bag. 'I've looked through Stan's diary covering my last year here. If you will look through the year following that it will save time and I can continue with his last one.'

'Precisely what do you want me to look for?'

'Any notes Stan has made apart from those to do with his gardening or birds,' he said.

She settled into a seat beside him and turned to the first page of January, promising, 'I'll check every page.'

Seated in companionable silence, Karenza became absorbed in the detailed records kept by Stan Collinson. And little else but the weather, the garden, and the birds were recorded, until she reached the beginning of May when she brought a note regarding a motor launch at anchor in the bay to Elliot's attention.

'Good. Check September as well, you may find a similar entry.'

Concentrating on the pages of September she gave Elliot a nudge. 'Hey, look at this!' she cried. 'It's about the motor launch and says, *No bathing or fishing observed. Tender came out from Rosecliffe,* and on the following day it says, *the launch had left during hours of darkness.* What do you make of that?'

'I'll tell you later. Meanwhile, put one of those strips of paper I gave you between the pages will you, Karenza? I may want to recheck those dates.'

'I can't understand why Stan should make a note about that launch after you told me he wasn't too keen on anything to do with the sea.'

'Ah yes, but the same launch was there around the time I was arrested.'

'Oh, Elliot, I hope you're not stirring up something that could be dangerous.'

'Take a look at this from last year and you will understand my interest.'

Karenza's eyes came to rest on where he drew his finger across the page of early September to see an entry about a launch similar to the one she had found in hers. But beneath it, in Stan's slightly shaky hand it said,

Evers and Latham on Rosecliffe, one way—boat? 5 p.m. tender loading on to launch. Left 6 p.m. Then, two days later, *Owner of Trewyn ill—hotel for sale?—must inform Elliot.*

'I find that quite upsetting to read as Stan died only five days later,' he told her, suppressing a lump that rose in his throat. Turning the page he held it open for her to see further entries, and on the facing page, *No digging today, my old ticker bothering me.* On the next day Latham was mentioned again, but on the next day following no word about gardening, only that he had pain in his chest.

'Poor Stan,' she murmured, 'keeping a diary until the day before he died. Do you think he meant Latham and Evers were over at Rosecliffe Hotel?'

Elliot frowned. 'I'm not sure about that. Some consider Rosecliffe as the whole cliff area from the village to a mile or more east of the hotel. Naturally, Stan would be able to observe a large part of it from his allotment up there and I'd very much like to know what was being loaded on to that launch.'

'I can't believe the hotel to be involved in anything suspicious, yet Mr Latham was there this evening.'

'Could be a coincidence,' he said, and yet when he recalled the snippets of conversation he'd overheard one morning he considered there was something very suspicious about that place.

'Not heard from the surveyor yet, have you?' she asked. 'It will soon be a week since he made a start.'

'Not quite a week. You are far too impatient.' Elliot laughed. 'Actually, you've just reminded me, I haven't got my mobile with me and it's the only number he has. I'll go over to the hotel early in the morning and pick it up from my room before I settle my account and collect my luggage.'

*   *   *

When Karenza came downstairs the next morning she found Elliot fast asleep. Tip-toeing into the kitchen she switched on the kettle ready to make a pot of tea, but it wasn't long before he appeared beside her.

'Good morning, darling,' he said sleepily and dropped a kiss on her cheek. 'I intended to be up and about before this.'

'I wanted to leave you until breakfast. Didn't you sleep well on that sofa?'

'Actually, it was very comfortable, but I was reading the diaries until three.'

'Did you learn anything more?'

'Yes,' he said, 'and according to Stan's entries the launch could appear in the bay any day now.'

'I noticed it always seemed to be May and September, I wonder why?'

He laughed. 'Maybe the crew are poor

sailors as I notice they don't risk crossing in the winter months. Mr Tresidder thought he had seen either a French or Belgian flag so I assume they cross the channel.'

'Elliot, don't you think it's time we brought this to the attention of the police?'

'Or the coastguard,' he suggested. 'I believe that was something Stan had in mind.' He sighed and added, 'Whatever we decide, I must go over to Rosecliffe to collect my luggage. They've had a good opportunity to check my room.'

Once Elliot had left Karenza began to prepare breakfast, when the telephone rang in the next room.

'Has Wilson gone?' the caller asked.

Karenza froze but didn't immediately reply. The faintly accented voice she heard sounded like that of the blonde-haired man who had called the previous day.

'Take my advice—think of the kid,' the caller continued harshly.

This alarmed Karenza. 'What has it got to do with him?' she demanded, her heart beginning to pound.

'Just get rid of Wilson, or else!'

Determined not to be intimidated, Karenza retorted, 'Don't you dare threaten me—I shall call the police!'

'If you do you will suffer, you and the kid, I'm warning you!'

Shocked by the threats, she slammed down

the receiver with a shaking hand then tried to locate the caller's number. But, as she expected, it had been withheld. A sob of fear caught in her throat—she must contact Elliot.

She gasped in relief when his car pulled up outside and she dashed to the door. 'Oh Elliot!' she cried, 'I was about to ring you . . .'

He hastened towards her. 'Darling, what is it? What has happened?'

'That blond man again,' she blurted out. 'I'm sure it was him.'

'Let's go inside,' he suggested, urging her back into the house.

'It was the same voice,' she gasped. 'He threatened both Tom and I will suffer unless you go . . . oh, Elliot, what am I going to do?'

'And what else had he to say?' he prompted, his expression grim.

Overcome by distress she hid her face against his chest. 'Just get rid of Wilson. He said, think of the kid, inferring he would harm him.'

'I see,' Elliot said calmly. 'Oh, Karenza, can't you see that if you take notice of these threats the caller has accomplished what he set out to do.'

Tears sprang to her eyes once more, and her voice trembled as she reminded him, 'But it wasn't only me he threatened. Tom is in danger, too!'

'Please believe me, Karenza, I won't allow anyone to harm either of you, and I don't intend to leave you alone for one moment. Even so, I'm beginning to think I should bring this to the attention of the police.'

'Perhaps you should, Elliot, but I'll feel safer if you are here.'

'That's my girl!' he responded cheerfully. 'I thought we could go across the beach this morning, round the cliff side to the area under Rosecliffe Hotel,' he proposed. 'I want to see what is below the notice warning people not to venture too close.'

'The tide will be coming in, you'll get wet.'

'Then we go prepared to paddle, or even swim,' he said, 'though I don't expect a high tide.'

'I believe the cliff overhangs a little there, so it could be dangerous,' she told him.

'The sooner we get away the fewer people will be around as we may have to remove our clothes if the water's high.'

Karenza gave a short laugh. 'We did say we would go for a swim so why not today! After we've eaten I'll put a couple of towels and my costume in a bag.'

Walking hand in hand along the beach they soon came to the point where the water reached the outcrop of rock, but only gentle ripples surged in which meant the tide was most likely on the turn.

'Shouldn't be too deep but I suggest we put our shoes and trousers in my bag,' Elliot said. 'I'd hate to get back and find our clothes missing.'

With their belongings in the bag, Elliot hooked a finger under the handles and slung it over his shoulder. With his other hand he held Karenza to help her keep her balance as they waded knee deep round the point through rather chilly water. 'Take care,' he said. 'There are a few sharp rocks amongst this sand.'

'If we had gone farther out to avoid them we would have to swim and it's a bit too chilly for that this morning.'

'Later, when the sun is high,' he suggested, squeezing her hand.

'You still haven't told me why we are paddling round here. What, or who, do you expect to see?' she asked nervously.

'After what Mr Tresidder told me, it seems there are a few underground passages leading to the cliff from the cellars of some old houses. Rosecliffe has cellars, maybe they exit under the cliff. This is what I hope to find out.'

They walked over the seaweed and round to a beach she had not been on before. It was a small sheltered cove of clean golden sand stretching back to the rocky face of the cliff, and unless one was willing to paddle at low tide it appeared to be accessible only by way of the rough steps cut into the cliffside. A short distance from these steps they saw two overturned boats sheltered by tangled bushes.

Dropping the bag to the sand, Elliot moved over to the boats, examining the blue painted one first before moving along to the other which was the larger of the two and the colour of port wine. It was then that she heard his gasp of surprise and moved quickly towards him.

'Look at this!' he cried. 'Its name is *Trewyn*, so I can guess where it belongs.'

'What on earth is it doing here!' she exclaimed. 'I wonder if someone up in the hotel can tell you.'

He gave a short laugh. 'I'm sure they can! It appears to have been used only recently, but I won't mention it until I've spoken to the agent,' he said. 'Also, I'd like to see the inventory first.' Suddenly, aware his mobile was ringing he dashed over to the bag he had left on the sand.

Karenza heard him exclaim, 'What a coincidence, you're just the man I want!'

Strolling towards the cliffside, she waited until he had taken the call. But as she drew near to where the abundant greenery sprouted from between the rocks she saw what looked like a rough wooden door.

'Elliot, look!' she cried. 'It looks like a door behind these bushes.'

Returning his phone to the bag he went towards the place she indicated. 'So there is, and it's very secure,' he agreed, trying to get a finger hold in the heavy wood. And letting the tangled greenery fall back to conceal the door, he added, 'I expect it leads to the cellars, just as Tresidder described. By the way, that was the agent. He tells me the survey has been completed so I've agreed to meet him at *Trewyn* at half-past-two this afternoon. If all is in order we will continue on to his office in Truro.' Looking directly into her eyes, he stated, 'I would prefer you to come with me as I don't want to leave you alone.'

Glancing at his watch, Elliot pulled off his tee shirt and drew her towards him. 'Tell you what, Karenza, why don't we have a swim now? The air has warmed up considerably since the sun came out. All we shall need is a quick shower and change, and we can have a snack at that inn again on our way to Trewyn.'

They went hand in hand into the sea where the chill of the water momentarily took their breath away. And as they swam farther out he turned and trod water, pointing in the direction of the area way beyond the cliff top to tell her, 'That was Stan's allotment up there, at the very top of the hill. He had a good view of the sea but not the beach we've just been on. From up there it would be hidden by the cliff.' He reached out to float her towards him and kissed her wet cheek. 'Shall we go back now?'

She came up beside him, and lifting her from the water he carried her up the beach to set her down on a flat stone. She hugged him and looked up to see a sparkle in his dark eyes. She then gave a gasp of alarm when over

Elliot's shoulder she spotted someone on the cliff top. But as though the observer wished to avoid being seen he quickly drew back.

Elliot felt her stiffen in his arms and turned to look. 'What is it, Karenza?'

'There was a man in the grounds of Rosecliffe looking down on us,' she whispered, 'but I didn't recognise who it was.'

'Just someone strolling round the gardens I expect, taking in the view.'

'But I remember seeing a fence there and a warning to guests to keep clear.'

'So there was, but I expect it was one of the gardeners, they'd know the risk.'

She wrinkled her nose. 'Perhaps, but he seemed to be watching us.'

He laughed. 'Karenza, you must not let your imagination run riot. I'm sure lots of people like to take in the view from up there. I'm going to take a picture of this boat as proof of its whereabouts just in case it is the one from *Trewyn*,' he explained. 'And I see it's had an outboard motor.'

She nodded and stooped to put her wet costume into the bag, but as she straightened she spotted a red and white cigarette packet that had been discarded beside one of the boats. 'Elliot, look!' she cried, 'It's the same pack as the one I picked up by the gate at *Trewyn*.'

CHAPTER NINE

When they entered the inn where they lunched on their previous visit to *Trewyn*, Elliot's eyes were drawn to the framed photographs on the wall. 'I'd like to have a copy of these,' he said, 'and a book on *Trewyn*'s history if it's available.'

'Perhaps the landlord will know . . .' Karenza began just as the man in question appeared behind the bar to greet them.

'Good day to you, sir, and you, madam,' he said. 'What will you have?'

'A glass of wine, Karenza?' Elliot asked. 'I'll stick with orange.'

'There's fresh local crab on the menu today, sir.'

'I'd love a crab salad,' Karenza said as she took her glass of wine.

'And I'll forego a pasty for once and have the same,' Elliot grinned as they made their way to a table.

'You be staying in these parts?' the landlord enquired once he had their order.

'This lady lives in Porthaven,' Elliot replied with a glance at Karenza. 'But as for myself, I'm not sure how long I shall be around.'

'So you're not honeymooners, then?' the man asked with a twinkle in his eyes.

Elliot reached for Karenza's hand. 'No, but

I hope that day isn't too far away.'

'But from your accent I know you're a visitor.'

Elliot nodded. 'Actually, I'm on my way to *Trewyn* as you set me thinking the other day, and I've been making enquiries about the place.'

'Ah, yes,' the man said, his expression brightening as he continued, 'I had the agent who is dealing with *Trewyn* in here only yesterday. He mentioned that somebody from the north was interested. But during the last couple of days I hear there has been some activity around the place.'

'Would-be buyers do you mean?'

'Vandals is more like it,' the man snorted. 'However, I reported it to the police.' Then, with a lift of his shoulders, he corrected himself by adding. 'Well, not I exactly as the bar was busy just then, but soon after that Percy Latham and Evers came in so he offered to do it for me on his mobile.'

Karenza looked up in surprise. 'Really? I didn't realise Mr Latham got about much. He always moans he's too busy to leave the shop.'

'Oh yes, he calls in here regular on his half-day closing. I believe he has a bit of business over by the river.'

'Fishing you mean?' Elliot queried casually. 'I suppose it will be something relaxing for him to do after being tied to the shop all day.'

The landlord laughed. 'I don't think Percy is

patient enough for that. He be more interested in boats than fish—does a bit of sailing, I hear.'

Elliot absorbed this news with interest but merely nodded as he replied, 'A very pleasant pastime, I'm sure.'

Aware of Elliot's interest even though he appeared outwardly calm, Karenza concentrated on her meal. But immediately after they had finished their lunch and returned to the car he turned to her with a smile.

'What do you make of that? Latham doesn't sound like the harassed shopkeeper he would have you believe him to be.'

Karenza shook her head. 'As I said, this is the impression he gave, but now to hear he and Evers were in here together, well that is something else!'

'Mmm, I suspected something odd about these two,' he said thoughtfully as he started the engine. 'And by the comments in Stan's diaries I believe he also had his suspicions so perhaps I should take another look at his notes.'

On arriving at *Trewyn*, they saw the agent was already there, striding across from between the trees at the far end of the grounds, and when he glanced up Elliot noticed he appeared decidedly agitated.

'I wonder what has gone wrong,' Elliot said quietly as they waited for the agent to draw near.

'I'm having trouble with the boathouse,' the agent declared as he joined them. 'It appears the place had been cleaned out.'

'Yes, I told you there wasn't a boat in there, only packing materials, and a hose,' Elliot reminded him. 'But I see you've now got a key to the place.'

'Had a locksmith out—waste of time—wish I'd known about it earlier.'

'I thought it rather odd that you weren't even aware of the boathouse.'

The agent looked embarrassed. 'Those details were not to hand on your first visit,' he admitted, 'I had to rely on an old colleague of mine to correct that omission.'

'But what about the boat,' Karenza put in, 'you haven't mentioned that.'

The agent shook his head. 'It does appear on the inventory, I've checked, but until I spoke to you earlier I had no idea of its whereabouts.'

Elliot smiled. 'I may be able to help you with that,' he offered. 'If I can have the use of a computer you will see from the pictures in my camera that a boat bearing the name *Trewyn* lies upturned on a beach not too far away and it's my guess it belongs here.'

'Can you describe it?' the agent asked. 'Don't know too much about boats myself, but on the list I have it is described as a maroon-painted dinghy with outboard engine, plus buoyancy aids and fishing gear.'

'That's the one, same colour as the boathouse doors,' Elliot confirmed, 'but it had no outboard when we discovered it on the beach below Rosecliffe Hotel, though it appeared to have been at sea quite recently.'

'Don't forget the footprints,' Karenza put in. 'There were two sets.'

The agent nodded. 'The proprietor of the village inn told me he'd heard some activity and says one of his customers called the police. And yet, when I rang the local police yesterday evening they informed me it was the first they'd heard of it. They came out to investigate and found the boathouse doors open and the place totally empty.'

'Perhaps we should inform the police about the boat,' Elliot suggested.

'Leave it with me,' the agent said. 'I'll let them know tomorrow what you have discovered.'

'Now that has been settled shall we get down to business?' Elliot said.

Once a price had been agreed and a date set for a further meeting, Elliot and Karenza set off to go for a leisurely drive before returning home.

'We have a lot of planning to do, Karenza,' he said as he followed her into the cottage. 'But before anything is signed I want you to be sure that what I am proposing . . .' he broke off when the telephone rang and Karenza went to answer it. But by the tone of her voice he realised it was a friendly call and relaxed.

'They're coming home tomorrow!' she cried excitedly. 'Evidently it has been raining hard up there and the site is terribly muddy.' She sighed happily and reached for his hand. 'And what do you think Tom said,' she began, then seeing Elliot's bemused expression told him, 'he wants to come home to meet you.'

Elliot smiled. 'That's nice but how does he know about me?'

'I told him about you the last time we spoke, said you were a special friend. Anyway, Mum and Dad are looking forward to seeing you and hearing about *Trewyn*.'

'When are they due to arrive?'

'They're going to make an early start and have breakfast on the way, so should be here in time for lunch,' she told him. 'You will join us?'

'I think it will be better if I join you later— give you time to explain a few things.'

At breakfast the following morning, Elliot told her, 'I've found more notes in Stan's diary for last year. I read every single page and, if they keep to the same routine, that launch he refers to is due again tonight.'

'Tonight?' Karenza echoed in a startled voice. 'Are you certain?'

'It appears to be early May and September.'

'That's more than two years ago, but nothing before then?'

'No, I think it was my arrest which first brought it to Stan's notice. But I see there's a mention of him informing the coastguard last September before the launch left. According to Stan they had boarded it but appeared satisfied nothing was amiss.'

For a moment Elliot was silent, then he announced, 'Think I'll go and have a word with the coastguard this morning. Old Mr Tresidder as well.'

'But you will be coming back this afternoon?'

'Of course, darling, I'm looking forward to meeting everyone, but I'll give you a ring beforehand.'

Karenza had ample time to prepare a meal for the family's arrival so, because it was another warm day and the food wouldn't spoil, she made up a dish of cold meats to be served with a fresh salad.

As she lay back in the armchair afterwards, she smiled, her thoughts travelling over the past few days. How fortunate she was to have met up with Elliot again, and now Tom was a permanent member of the family she had everything her heart desired.

But whilst Karenza was relaxing, Elliot was down by the harbour telephoning the coastguard to voice his concerns. When he had completed the call, he uttered a sigh of frustration and walked over to Tresidder's cottage.

'Can you spare me a few minutes?' he asked the older man. 'You might know the best way for me to deal with this problem.'

'Come in, lad,' Tresidder invited before Elliot could continue. 'I was going to phone you. Something's happened this morning and I think you ought to know. I had a telephone call about an hour ago that may interest you,' Tresidder said, his eyes on his visitor as he began to stoke his pipe.

Elliot sat forward. 'May I ask, was it connected with *Trewyn*?'

The old man nodded and blew out a stream of smoke. 'Well, it was like this,' he began slowly, testing Elliot's patience, 'someone wanted to know if I had Stan Collinson's diaries.'

'Go on, Mr Tresidder,' Elliot urged. 'Do you know who the caller was?'

'No, I didn't recognise his voice. He spoke like that incomer who worked at *Trewyn*.'

'And where did he originate from, any idea?'

'Well, could be Amsterdam, but I've not been myself.' Tresidder chuckled.

'Mr Tresidder,' he began, taking the folded sheet of paper from his pocket. 'I've made more notes of Stan's entries in those diaries of his in the hope you can enlighten me. Also, I have had a word with the coastguard about the launch which, from Stan's notes, is due again tonight.'

Tresidder slapped his thigh and put down

113

his pipe. 'I knew there was something else I wanted to tell you. It's about that motor launch, it was here early this morning, I saw it in the bay,'

'You mean the same one Stan writes about?' Elliot interrupted, getting to his feet to move across to the small window.

'It's no good you looking, it isn't there now but I'd like to bet it will be back later,' the older man said, and nodded his head as he continued, 'Stan noticed they had changed tactics when last they were here.'

'That would be early September last year,' Elliot supplied eagerly.

'That's right, I went to see him on the allotment a few days before he died. He was looking through them binoculars of his. He told me he'd watched a fair haired fellow and a dark lad take a boat with an outboard out from Rosecliffe to the island, and later that day he'd spotted the launch heading in the same direction and they disappeared behind the rock.'

'So both vessels would be on the far side of the island?' Elliot surmised.

'That is exactly what we thought,' Tresidder nodded. 'Something was going on, that's for sure, but we couldn't decide what the launch could be bringing in, and after the coastguard declared it clean the last time, well . . .' he spread his hands in total bewilderment.

Karenza was still thinking about Elliot when

her father's car drew into the gateway. But Tom's screech of delight quickly alerted her and she dashed across the lawn to envelop him in her arms and kiss the top of his fair head.

'Hello, sweetheart,' she said, holding him at arms' length to look down on his tanned and smiling face. 'Have you had a lovely time?'

'Yes, but I want to see Elliot!' he cried eagerly. 'Is he here?'

'Hey, slow down a minute,' Karenza laughed.

Once the car boot had been emptied and everyone was settled in, contentedly sipping cups of tea, Tom looked up at Karenza to remind her, 'Are you going to tell me about him now?'

'As you are being such a good boy I'll tell you now.'

'I assume it concerns this friend of yours that you were telling me about the other day when I rang?' Mrs Rowe guessed.

Mr Rowe nodded. 'Yes, let's hear more about him.'

Karenza explained about Elliot to her father, but she was pleased he didn't reveal too much before Tom heard. Lifting the boy up on to her knee, she began, 'There is a very nice man staying in the village, Tom, and he likes being on the beach and swimming in the sea, and he also likes to go sailing.'

'Will he take me in his boat?' Tom broke in excitedly.

'He would like to meet you,' she told him, looking down on his eager little face, 'so you could ask him yourself.'

Once lunch was over and Tom had gone upstairs for a rest, Karenza and her mother washed the dishes whilst her father watched television in the sitting-room.

'I can tell you love Elliot very much,' Mrs Rowe said. 'And it sounds as though he will welcome our Tom.'

'Oh yes, Mum, I'm certain they will get on very well together,' Karenza assured her, glancing at her watch. 'As soon as Tom's awake we'll go down to the beach before it is time for Elliot to arrive. Would you like to come with us?'

'No thanks, I'm going to rest, but I'm so pleased your father and I had a little chat with you,' Mrs Rowe said, smiling, 'and we will look forward to meeting Elliot later this afternoon.'

About an hour later, Karenza found Tom already out of bed and struggling to put on his clothes. 'I think you should wear shorts for the beach,' she said, helping him pull the T-shirt over his head.

A delighted Tom grinned as he raced down the stairs towards the door. 'Wait whilst I get the towels,' she instructed. 'Do you want your bucket and spade?'

'Yes, Kenza,' he said, unable to pronounce her full Cornish name.

Karenza gave him a fond smile and they

116

were about to leave the house when her father appeared at the sitting-room door to say he had taken an urgent telephone message for her.

'It was that friend of yours, Elliot Wilson, he asked me to tell you to go down to the harbour where a boat will be waiting to take you to *Trewyn*.'

'Thanks, Dad, I wonder what he's doing at *Trewyn*?'

'Says he has some business to attend to, and he sounded in rather a hurry.'

'I'll take my mobile with me,' she said, 'then I can let you know if we are going to be late.'

CHAPTER TEN

With a happy child hanging onto her hand as he skipped along beside her, Karenza made her way down to the harbour. She wondered why Elliot had to go to *Trewyn* in such a hurry, but hoped it meant the purchase of the hotel was soon to be finalised. Arriving at the cobbled slope she met Doctor Smith who had just moored his boat after making an urgent call to one of his patients.

'You're back from holiday, I see,' he said giving Tom's nose a tweak.

'We are going on a boat,' Tom said proudly.

She laughed and related Elliot's message to

117

the doctor.

'Sorry I can't see you off,' he said. 'Be sure to wear your buoyancy aids.'

'Let's see if we can see this boat,' she said as the doctor hurried away.

On the far side of the jetty Karenza spotted a maroon boat not unlike the one she and Elliot had discovered on the cove below Rosecliffe Hotel.

'Miss Rowe!' called the man at the helm, beckoning her to join him. And as she hurried Tom along the jetty towards it she saw the name, *Trewyn*.

'I assume you are returning this boat to Trewyn? Elliot will be pleased.'

The man nodded. 'We must go now, Mr Wilson is waiting.'

'Of course, sorry. My nephew here is delighted to be going on a boat.'

'Pass him to me,' the man said, and taking Tom from her he sat him in the boat then held out a hand to assist her boarding.

'Oh yes, buoyancy aids,' she said once she was seated.

'You don't need buoyancy aids for that short trip,' the man smirked, and as she began to object she heard movement behind and felt the boat lurch away from the jetty. But when she turned to see who had joined them the engine accelerated and she almost lost her balance.

'There was no need for that!' she yelled,

making a grab for Tom to save him toppling from his seat. A faint sound of laughter came from close behind and she glanced back to see the blond-haired Evers, who had called at the cottage to ask for Stan's diaries. At first she was speechless as she realised she had been duped into believing she was on her way to meet Elliot at *Trewyn*.

Gathering courage, she said, 'I don't believe this is anything to do with Elliot Wilson so take me back now.'

Evers laughed even louder and the other one accelerated the engine so that they skimmed over the water at speed. She heard Tom give a nervous giggle and felt him cling more tightly to her hand.

She sent the child a quick smile and squeezed his hand as she addressed Evers to plead, 'Please, at least let me take the child back to Porthaven.'

'No way,' the man shot back, 'we'll do a better deal with two of you so keep quiet.' With a meaningful nod towards Tom he added, 'Otherwise . . .'

Karenza's heart sank as she quickly began to realise they were going in entirely the opposite direction to *Trewyn* and were now heading towards the small rocky island directly out from Rosecliffe. But where was Elliot?

*   *   *

119

Elliot organised bed and breakfast for himself at a farmhouse close to the Truro road where his car could be parked out of view. He went out to his car and called Karenza's home number, assuming she would be there.

But it was Mr Rowe who answered his call, explaining Karenza and Tom were out. But when Elliot introduced himself Mr Rowe became confused. 'Didn't you ring about an hour ago?' he asked. 'I gave her your message.'

'My message? Sorry, Mr Rowe, I don't understand.'

When Rowe repeated the message he had passed on to Karenza, Elliot felt the chill of fear grip his heart.

Considering it was pointless to worry the man further Elliot said, 'Don't worry, I'll go down to the harbour and when I find them I'll give you a call.' And with a screech of tyres he drove on to the main road to head for Porthaven.

Going downhill in the direction of the harbour he spotted Doctor Smith chatting with Mr Tresidder. Lowering his windows he called to them, 'Have you seen Karenza and Tom?'

The doctor frowned, 'Surely, you've just left her. She told me you were waiting for them at *Trewyn.* They were going by boat.'

Elliot's eyes widened in horror. 'Whose boat was that—did she say?'

'No, she didn't, but I can understand your anxiety. Mr Tresidder here has been telling me a few rather alarming facts.'

'Right, I'm going to *Trewyn* immediately,' Elliot decided and was about to turn the car round when the doctor suggested they would do better going by boat.

'You can come with me, it will be much faster, and I'll call the police,' Doctor Smith offered.

'I'll bring my binoculars,' Elliot decided. 'I should have expected something like this,' he groaned. 'Someone is determined to stop me purchasing *Trewyn*.'

'Apparently, you are getting in someone's way, but it's no good berating yourself, Elliot, we've pulled out all the stops. Does Karenza carry a mobile?'

'I think so, Doctor, I'll give her a call. But first, tell me what the police had to say? Are they going to meet up with us at *Trewyn*?'

'They didn't seem to think enough time has passed before they organise a search, but when I mentioned a child was involved they took it more seriously. They also pointed out that *Trewyn* may only have been used to obstruct our search and they could have gone entirely in the opposite direction.' The doctor glanced at Elliot to remind him sharply, 'You should be wearing a buoyancy aid—you would be no use to anyone if you fell in!'

'You're right,' agreed Elliot, pulling one from the locker.

Doctor Smith cast him an anxious glance. 'If

they're not at *Trewyn* we'll turn back and search along the coast,' he decided.

'I'll try giving her a call,' Elliot decided and keyed in the number without success, 'Strange,' he said, 'she's not answering.'

*   *   *

'Are we going to paddle now?' Tom asked as the boat threaded its way between the pinnacles of rock.

'Not just yet,' Karenza replied, deeply disappointed after having her mobile confiscated when it rang.

'Can we get out now?' Tom asked when he saw they were nearing the island.

'Soon,' Karenza replied calmly, and to Evers she said, 'Surely, you don't intend to leave us here?'

'You're going nowhere until we've persuaded Wilson to withdraw his offer for *Trewyn*,' he said, slotting the knotted mooring rope between the rocks before grabbing Tom to carry him over to the beach.

'He won't listen to you,' she retorted, then gasped as she stepped out of the boat into a foot or more of water. Tom started to cry.

'My bucket and spade,' he shouted and she slid her rucksack off her shoulder, then heard her mobile ring in Evers' hand.

'This will be Wilson,' he smirked, 'he's got two chances. Either he goes, or you and the kid.'

Karenza felt her heart sink as Evers walked away just as she caught Elliot's anxious voice. About to call out, she managed to stop herself when she saw him glance meaningfully at Tom.

'Wilson?' she heard Evers say, 'I hope you are paying attention. I am prepared to bring the boy back to Porthaven in exchange for your promise to withdraw your offer for *Trewyn.*'

By the man's expression it appeared Elliot was objecting when he uttered a curse and demanded, 'Ring me again, and make it soon or you could be too late!'

'Can I have my spade now?' she heard Tom ask. 'I want to dig in the sand.'

'You can dig for as long as you like, lad, once Wilson sees sense.'

'Look, you can't keep us here, my family will alert the police,' she said.

Evers merely grinned. 'We shall be gone from here long before the police put in an appearance,' he sneered, suddenly falling silent when there came a splash of oars from an approaching boat. To Karenza's surprise she saw the oarsman was the young chap who assisted Percy Latham, a plaster on the side of his face.

The newcomer appeared both excited and frightened as he rushed towards the two men to cry out a few words in French. 'We must go!' she translated, but saw Evers shrug and ask his companion, 'What's he on about?'

The young man continued to speak very quickly, and Karenza got the gist of this almost hysterical message brought from the launch to say they had finished loading, but they suspected a patrol boat might be taking an interest and wanted to get away.

Karenza was more scared than ever before in her life yet she had to protect Tom who in his innocence was playing happily with the stones. 'Please, let us go,' she begged. 'You'll frighten the child.'

'Doesn't look too frightened to me,' Evers sneered as he lit a cigarette from a familiar red and white soft pack, then turning to his companion he urged, 'Give the youth his instructions, we'll be off!'

Evers then went to start the engine of the boat named *Trewyn* whilst his colleague spoke to the younger man in the language they shared. She understood him to say, 'Watch them—we'll be back for you,' as he joined Evers in the boat.

About to protest, she quickly realised it would be wiser for her to pretend not to understand what was happening.

It was when Tom was making an effort to write his name that she had an idea. She wrote her own name on a flat rock and asked the youth in French for his name. At first he simply stared in amazement, then delighted to hear his own language he smiled and said,

'Jules,' and scratched his name beneath hers.

'I don't believe they will come back for you, Jules,' she warned in her hesitant French and met his anxious eyes. 'They spoke in English so that you wouldn't understand, said they wanted to leave before the patrol boat comes back.'

Jules moved away, scrambling over the rocks to reach a higher point where he could see if the launch was still at anchor on the other side of the tiny island. Hardly daring to make a sound she watched Jules disappear from sight and knew this may be their only chance to attempt an escape.

'Tom, come with me,' she hissed, lifting him off his feet to dash for the blue boat which bobbed up and down in the waves. Wading almost thigh deep through the water she swung Tom over the side and flung herself in after him, using an oar to push the boat clear of the rocks.

Relieved to find the tide was taking them quickly away from the island, she wondered if the two men would return in the other boat, or had they left Jules to find his own solution? She almost felt sorry for the youth.

Elliot was relieved to see the police arrive at *Trewyn*. 'Any news?' he enquired as they clambered over.

The constable shook his head and asked, 'You here alone?'

'No, Doctor Smith from Porthaven is with

me, his boat is on the river by the boathouse,' said Elliot.

'I see, so you're the chap from Scotland. Mr Tresidder mentioned you.'

'Yes, did he also tell you I was here over two years ago?'

'As a matter of fact he did and I clearly remember your case.' He shook his head and with a smile continued, 'At the time I felt really sorry for you.'

'Well, I'm in a much worse situation now. As we said when we rang, those men threatened to hold Miss Rowe and the boy until I agree to withdraw my offer for this place, so I need some advice on what to do next.'

'How are you supposed to make contact with them.'

'He's got Karenza's mobile, he's waiting for my call,' Elliot replied. 'Incidentally, Mr Wilson, have you had a look in the cellars?'

'No, officer, I haven't the key. I can ring the agent if you like, although I've been given to understand the cellars have been emptied and closed up.'

'But not for as long as you may think. We suspect there has been illegal traffic in the area again and they'll shift anything, antiques, jewellery, forged notes . . .'

'Only yesterday Karenza and I discovered the boat that belongs to *Trewyn* in that small cove beneath Rosecliffe Hotel and, by the looks of it, it had been out that morning,' Elliot told him. 'I took photographs to prove it.'

The policeman soon suggested they join Doctor Smith on his boat.

The second officer had gone ahead and was already speaking to the doctor. 'It was the vicar from Porthaven who reported seeing two boats go out from Rosecliffe,' he related. 'He was taking his dogs along the beach when these boats came from behind the cliff, both appearing to be laden with goods.'

'Yes, he told me about that,' the doctor put in. 'And since some artefacts had gone missing from the church it made him suspicious.'

'And not only from this church,' the first officer added. 'There had been another spate of thefts from a number of country houses in the south.'

Elliot interrupted. 'I'm terribly worried about Karenza and the boy!'

'Call that mobile, convince them you are in the process of withdrawing your offer. Ask to speak to the lady they're holding, or the child, and persuade them to name a pick-up place,' the policeman said.

Karenza was beginning to feel exhausted, but when she looked down on Tom's trusting smile she was spurred on to continue using one oar. And yet, as fast as she tried to pull it through the water, the boat seemed to be veering towards the island again.

127

Pulling the pink towel from her bag she decided to use it as a flag to give them a better chance of being spotted. But she had to find a way of securing it to the remaining oar. Drawing the oar into the boat she pulled the drawstring from the waistband of Tom's shorts and secured the towel to it.

'What are you doing, Kenza?' he asked.

'I'm making a flag for our boat,' she said, and felt the pain of unshed tears constricting her throat when she saw the admiration in his eyes.

Elliot climbed back into Doctor Smith's boat and they left *Trewyn* behind to head for the open sea, hoping to spot Karenza and Tom somewhere along the coast.

'I felt sorry for the agent,' the doctor remarked. 'To have been led to believe the cellars were no longer in use must have made him feel foolish.'

'The packing materials in there were of the same type I had seen in the boathouse, and it seems this sort of smuggling has been going on for some time,' Elliot sighed.

As they passed the cove below Rosecliffe Hotel there was no sign of either boat, so Elliot concentrated on the beaches farther along until the doctor swung his boat to starboard, heading out in the direction of the island.

Suddenly Elliot spotted a familiar maroon boat, but today it had a powerful looking outboard motor fitted, its propeller raised clear of the shingle. 'Can we go in, Doctor? That looks like the boat from *Trewyn*!'

'Yes, we'll take a look, though you will have to paddle if you want to get closer,' the doctor warned.

Karenza's arms felt as though they would break. She was beginning to wonder if they would ever be rescued though she didn't dare to relax like Tom who had dropped off to sleep again. As she flexed her aching muscles she thought she heard the throb of an engine.

Quickly alert, she raised the oar again, clenching her teeth as she felt the wind pull at her makeshift flag.

The engine sounds were growing louder now and seemed to be coming from her left. Then, only moments later she saw the bow of a boat nose its way round the island. She could see two members of crew, one of them appearing to be holding binoculars before his eyes. She knew immediately it was Elliot.

Waving wildly, she cried out his name. And as she realised the boat belonged to Doctor Smith a white flare shot into the air.

Moments later she saw Elliot remove some of his clothes before he leapt into the sea and started swimming towards them with powerful strokes.

As Karenza swung her legs over the side to reach Elliot's outstretched hands another boat came round the island at speed. Throwing up spray as it swung round, one of its occupants, a coastguard, came to join Elliot who had Karenza and Tom held tightly in his arms.

'Don't worry, Doctor Smith is calling your parents to let them know you're safe,' Elliot said.

'The police are taking the gang into custody, including Latham,' the coastguard informed Elliot, and to Karenza he said, 'We'll get you two back to the boat and let the doctor have a look at you.'

'I want to go with Elliot,' Tom piped up.

'OK,' agreed Elliot. 'Put on this life jacket, I'll tow you.'

'What about Kenza?' Tom asked and Elliot laughed.

'Don't you worry about Karenza,' he said gently. 'I can look after you both.' And giving the boy a hug he added, 'And we can all live at *Trewyn*.'